the
Life
and
Loves
of
Mr.
Jiveass
Nigger

This is for
Dorothy, Aileen, and Donald

the
Life
and
Loves
of

Mr.
Jiveass
Nigger

Farrar, Straus & Giroux
New York

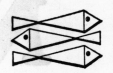

a
novel
by

Cecil

Brown

contents

Contents

*the
Life
and
Loves
of
Mr.
Jiveass
Nigger*

prologue

A Prismatic Account of Some
Important Matters

one *The Spirit of the Father*

I swear 'fo God this is the cussinges' man ever born, he must've been cussing when he came into this world, when his mother, Miss Lillybelle Washington, gave birth to this heathen the first thing he said must've been a cuss word, he probably cussed out the midwife and his mother and anybody else who happened to be in sight, cussed them out for bringin' him into the world, he is that kind of man, you know. . . . There ain't a soul in this community he ain't cussed out, hardly a dog or cat either. But the Lord is gonna visit this nigger, you watch and see, he's gonna visit this nigger. When I met him, when I first laid eyes on this nigger he was cussing, out in the street cussing with my brothers, and I said to myself, why is that nigger always using cuss words? So I thought it was just youth, just being young, and I was foolish enough to up and marry that fool. He tole me after we got married he was gonna stop cussing, and you know the stranges' thing is that he did. And three months later, he cuss old man Lennon into a blue streak. Old man Lennon ain't never bother no body, that old man been walking around this town for forty years picking up junk in his wheelbarrow and taking it home to see what use he could fine out of it, and he happened to come by the house and this nigger of mine claimed the man picked up his hammer. Lord God Almighty, did he cuss that poor man out. I can't stand no cussing man, I don't like no cussing man, Lord gib me any kind of man, a short, square-headed man, a ugly man, any kind of man, but don't give me no cussing man. I got experience to prove this: that there ain't but one thing a cussing man is good for and that is cussing. There is one thing about a cussing man that you can bet your bottom dollar on and that is he will cuss, and if he don't cuss, grits ain't grocery, eggs ain't poultry, and Mona Lisa was a man. But the Lord gonna visit that nigger, the Lord, or somebody, gonna visit him, because you can't go through life cussing out everybody, everything you see, you just can't do that, and get away with it. Or am I a fool? That nigger cussed out God himself, yes he did. I was telling him he should go to church, you know once in a while, not all the time, just once in a while, and that nigger broke bad and said that the Lord could kiss his black ass. But the Lord ain't gonna kiss no nigger's black ass, or if he do kiss it then that nigger knows something I don't know and wanna find out about pretty quick. My grandmother, Dennier Saint Marie, she's dead and gone now, she tole me when I was nothing but a five-year-old. Tole me to never marry a cussing man. One of her boyfriends, she had aplenty, she had three children by black men and three by white men, and some by an Indian too (we got all kinds of blood in us), one of her boyfriends, who use to wear that straw hat that put you in the mind of a tap dancer, he had just come into the gate and we was all sitting on the porch, it was a Sunday afternoon, and there was some white and red roses in the garden and we had picked some red roses and pinned them to our clothes in honor of the fact that our mother was alive, it was Easter Sunday you know and Gramma had a white one for her blouse, and this boy-friend of hers came bursting into the gate, just cussing like a nigger, I mean he was *talking*, but every few words was a cuss word, and Gramma just turned politely to him and said would you excuse yourself, there's some ladies present, and he said you never heard shit before, everybody shits, and Gramma said you better get your filthy ass out of this garden. And when he left, she turned to me (it seems like she was speaking only to me even though there were about twelve people present) and said, honey don't ever marry a cussing man, because a cussing man ain't good for nothing but one thing—and that's cussing. Now those was some words I should have heeded, but I didn't heed them, I went right out and the first man I looked at good I married (because I loved him) and he turned out to be a cussing man. I don't care what my sons be, I don't care really what they do, just so they don't grow up cussing everything they lay eyes on. I can't stand no cussing man. When I hear a man cussing, my insides go to pieces. That's one thing about white men. They shor don't cuss like niggers. Of course, a poor white peck will cuss. A poor white peck will cuss worse'n a nigger. I am talking about white men who ain't poor like them pecks. I guess a nigger man cuss because he is so poor and ain't nothin' but a nigger. But a nigger should learn not to cuss, he should learn not to cuss too much. To tell you the truth, there ain't nothin' wrong with cussing, I do a little bit myself, but there is somethin' wrong with a nigger cussing *all the time*. There is somethin' wrong with that kind of nigger, somethin' done gone wrong deep down inside of that nigger, if everything he says is a blasphemous cuss word, if every time he opens his mouth it's a cocksucker, motherfucker-down-the-ditch-up-the-ditch-longheaded-sonofabitch, or if he is always saying, I wish I was dead, I'm gonna be glad when I die (like some niggers I know), and things like this, then there is something deep down wrong with that nigger and he oughta go to church and testify. But this man won't testify, he above testifying, he rather cuss, I guess cussing is his way of testifying. I can understand that, I just hope God understands it.

When George's mother married his father she was fifteen and a very fine woman. She was probably one of the finest women in the world. George's father was a young, strong black man when he married the woman, but he had one fault which the woman grew to resent very strongly, and that was that he cursed. It was true too that he cursed all the time. It was also a contagious thing. If you were around George's father you would be cursing too without even really knowing it. George tried not to curse. He tried very hard, and he was very good at it. He could talk whole sentences without cursing once, and then he could hold a conversation with almost anybody (that is to say, any adult) without cursing, and finally he was able to talk a whole day without saying a curse word—or at least he thought he could; that is to say, it seemed so to *him*. Once, however, in the classroom, Ellen accused him of calling her a curse name, which for the life of him he could not remember having said. He turned to Reb for verification, and Reb slowly shook his head affirmatively, indicating that indeed he had spoken a curse word. He could not believe that he was that unconscious of himself. And yet there was Reb looking disappointed and sad because he had to tell the truth. But no! he had not cursed, it was his father speaking through him, speaking through him unconsciously. He began to hate his father who was buried deep inside of him and who was a nigger and cursed all the time. He began to hate the uncon-

scious part of himself. He tried to be conscious of every single thing that he did; he wanted to be conscious of every
single reaction he had on people, and when he thought that
people reacted to something in him which he himself did not
recognize or know he became uncomfortable.

And worst of all his father wanted George to become a
lawyer or doctor, and George knew he wanted this, so that
when George was five or six and went to visit him in prison,
George said to him, I think I'll be a lawyer or doctor or
something like that. His father's thin black face yielded
a white set of teeth. But did George Washington become a
lawyer or doctor, or something like that? No, he became a
hustler, a jiveass, a jazz player who could never quite get the
kind of versatility to match the humming in his head, a well-
read hanger-on, a poet without the appropriate metaphors.
Yeh, didn't he head straight for Harlem when he graduated
from high school, throwing away a scholarship to a good
Negro college only a hundred and fifty miles away, threw it
away because he thought the college was inferior to his in-
nate ability and would hence hamper his growth? But what
did he do instead? Did he attend a better college in the
North? No. He just sat around thinking that if he had gone
to Princeton, like his friend Randall, he'd have done extremely well, because Randall was not so bright and he did
all right. Sat around and even invented a myth of himself at
Princeton, calling the myth Paul Winthrop, Jr. Paul Winthrop, Jr., was the most well-read Princetonian to walk the
campus in many years, especially knowledgeable on English
literature of the period 1590–1600.

And the myth of Julius Makewell, the original nigger—ex-
gorilla (who actually came on that way). SCENE: *an attrac-*

tive blonde like the one right out of the Dodge Rebellion television commercial, sitting in a fire-red Fiat. Enter from the left wing (125th Street), JULIUS: *hair not combed in weeks, standing twisted on his head in a million different directions, eyes weird and red from wine.*

JIVEASS NIGGER ALIAS GEORGE WASHINGTON ALIAS JULIUS MAKEWELL: Hey, gimme a ride.

GIRL: Where you going?

JULIUS: Where you going? Updown Downtown Eastside Westside?

GIRL: Uh . . . okay, sure . . . if you promise not to . . . (*Cut to:* GIRL's *bedroom. A big large bed with impressive wooden frame. Poster of Eldridge Cleaver on one wall and Martin Luther King on another. Both* JULIUS *and* GIRL *sit on bed.*)

GIRL: So that's it. That's all you want, huh? Is that why you say you're coldblooded? You mean, you want to just . . . as you said, screw me, just like that, huh? Without even having any idea of what I'm like at all. Just walk right in and stick it in, huh? Is that the kind of person you are, is it?

JULIUS (*sheepish*): Yes.

GIRL (*exasperated*): You mean, you don't even wanna know my name? You don't even care who I am at all?! You mean you can do that—walk right off the street and into bed??

JULIUS (*painfully*): Yes.

GIRL: Jesus Christ, what kind of person are you?

JULIUS (*seriously attempting an explanation*): I've been this way . . . (*He glances at the* GIRL's *legs, which are opened and uncovered by her micro-mini*) . . . been this way all my life. (*Turns to the audience, and in an aside*): Yeah, I guess this is what it means to be a Negro.

GIRL (*very sympathetic*):   It must be a terrible way to be!

JULIUS: I just have to do it. (*His hands caress the* GIRL's *most available thigh and then move farther up.*)

GIRL: Oh, I understand . . . (*Panting with excitement*) . . . but you don't think you could wait . . . until . . . I mean, we've only known each other ten minutes . . .

JULIUS (*caressing* GIRL):   I've always been this way. I—I just can't help it.

GIRL: Well, is that all you want?

JULIUS: This is all I want.

GIRL: Just my body?

JULIUS (*sheepish*):   Uh, yes.

GIRL: You don't even want to know my name?!

JULIUS: We went through this once—NO!

GIRL (*thoughtfully*):   Well, if *that's* the way you want it, okay. (*Begins panting again as she takes off clothes.*) Sure you . . . don't wanna know my name.

JULIUS: No. This is a one-day stand. I'll never see you again.

GIRL: Okay . . . if this is what you want . . . (*Undresses.*)

(*Fade into darkness.*)

And you don't go to sleep afterwards, and you think about the TV, the radio, the ring, the watch, and the $32.89 in her handbag, but what can she really complain about. 'Cause I ain't got shit in this world. Yo' daddy got it all, baby!

And anything else he could grab onto. Any other myth of the self. And lying to himself, successfully selling overpriced

*encyclopedias to illiterate black people in the slum tene-
ments of Brooklyn and Harlem and hustling and flimflamming a 250-pound woman preacher in Harlem for all she
was worth. Lies. Yeh, yeh. Why? Why? Why?*

two *A Brief History*

Let us backtrack a moment. The most salient characteristic of George Washington's early childhood (and, indeed, his early youth) was his *individuality*. This talent of his, the almost fanatical ability to remain *different* against all odds, was apparent even at birth: young George Washington was born on the Fourth of July in the year of Our Lord nineteen hundred and forty-four in his father's bed, which had been recently vacated by George's grandfather, who had to flee the county for having (allegedly) whipped a fellow—Josh Smith, to be exact—with a slab because the said Josh had accused George's grandfather of having fathered a child by Josh's poor wife. George was assisted in entering this world by his grandmother, a squatty little woman with very definite strains of Indian blood, who will swear to this day that when George Washington came out of the womb he was grinning. No one knew what he was grinning about. Except, of course, George himself. His grandmother claimed he was the blackest baby she'd ever seen come into the world, and later on, when George was older, she went on to offer the opinion that he was the *blackest child she'd ever seen period*. There is some truth in this, for the child was extremely dark, and it was this unusual hue that led many members of the family to think that he was destined to become, as it were, the black sheep of the family. But the most amazing change occurred to George when he was in the last of his fifth year: his skin began to get lighter, until, at age twelve, he possessed the finest shade of brown complexion imaginable, and it was this complexion that he kept for the balance of his days. No one really understood why the change took place at the time that it did, or really what it signified. It is, however, a small matter, and besides it is only his mother and grandmother who still insist that George Washington was once *really* black. His mother, furthermore, is very pleased with the brown hue of her first-born.

When George was only two, his father, Jake, who, incidentally, was the one who earmarked him with the name George, went off to prison, in very much the same fashion as some young fathers were at that time going off to war—that is to say, reluctantly. With the exception of brief visits, George did not see his father for a great number of years, but he was not without a father figure. Quite to the contrary, young Washington lived in a household that was abounding with male models: his four uncles, ranging from age seventeen to twenty-eight, who shared the house with the rest of the family (twelve or thirteen or fourteen, depending on whether you counted Buckcaesar or Siren as dogs or humans), were very excellent models, indeed. Illiterate, generous, intuitive, simple, and hopelessly backwards, they were probably some of the finest men in the whole world. From them little Washington learned at an exceptionally early age how to swear, talk about women, talk *to* women, how to farm, hunt, fish, avoid unnecessary work, how to relax, how to tell when a white cracker is trying his best to get something for nothing (which is most of the time), and how to look at a nappy head woman and tell if the sap's running. Like all true students, George outgrew his teachers and became something his uncles never dreamed of: he became literate, which is to say, he became a voracious reader of any piece of printed matter he could lay hands on. Because he was such a lover of reading, and being the only one in the household who could read (with the exception of his mother), it was his task and pleasure to read any bit of mail, be it a letter from Aunt Mabel in Philly or third-class advertisement sheets, aloud for all to hear, in very much the fashion of the town crier. He was much appreciated by the family for his learning and gentlemanly bearing, and was much loved by all. And thus he spent his early years until the age of twelve, at which point he was (un)fortunately seduced by a wayward and voluptuous aunt. After this initial loss of innocence, the boy took to laying out with women, and to heavy usage of rot-gut liquor, cigarettes, and reefers. When he was only eight, his teacher once asked the class who the father of our country was, and of course George was quick to shout out his name—proudly. In a brief five years, however, all this optimism was shot to hell, for George's most favorite expression of his philosophical view of life was summed up in a conscious parody of Ecclesiastes' famous dictum: "I have seen all the works that are done under the sun; and, behold, all *is* jive and vexation of the spirit." Many a night he lay his gun down on an oak, and stared up at the stars and, wondering what it all meant, lost his consciousness in a spiritual transcendence that would leave him shivering and scratching about, two hours later, for his soul. Upon recovering, he would chant, "Jive, it's all jive."

In high school, George had a sidekick named Reb. Reb was mean and slick, which was why George liked him. The last thing George saw of Reb was the back of his straw hat. The two of them were sitting in the principal's office, waiting for the baldheaded sonabitch to peep his head in the door. Reb had a mallet and George had a piece of pine slab. Reb's fine straw hat was cocked to the side, and sweat was trickling down his brown forehead. George was a little

scared too. After Reb leveled on that nigger principal's head
with that mallet, he broke out and ran. The last thing
George saw was the back of his straw hat. Then, five years
later, George came back to Royaltown to visit. He had been
up in Harlem flimflamming a colored woman preacher out
of $935 and thought he would take a little vacation. He
wanted to see his family again and where he grew up. So
here he was back home. He went to the high school to see
his brother play basketball. The place had not changed. He
saw an extremely attractive girl sitting watching his little
brother shoot some perfect shots into the basket and he went
over to the girl and as it turned out she was Reb's wife and
she said Reb was in the army in Vietnam, that he was a
sergeant, had been decorated, and that he didn't want to kill
any more Vietnamese people but that he didn't have any
choice but as soon as he could get out of it he was going to,
which was in June. And George thought that the girl was
extremely attractive and Reb was very fine and then he
thought of Reb in a foxhole somewhere in that lonely country and he was sad but then he said to the girl that he had
grown up with her husband and that she shouldn't worry
because Reb was going to survive because he was a beautiful, jiveass nigger. George did not believe the girl understood his last phrase. Three days after that he was in Copenhagen.

*And in final desperation you fling yourself on a plane and
land in a city named Copenhagen. You want to know why it
is that you tell so many lies. Do other people lie like this? Is
there any motherfucker in this despiteful world who ever
told himself the truth? You want to know. And so, your story
opens:*

the tale

one

The Strøget, Copenhagen's Fifth Avenue, must be, during the summer months, one of the finest streets in the world. No cars are permitted on this street, which means one can interweave freely, provided he is careful not to step on one of the hundreds of street artists whose nearly bad drawings always draw coins from the patronizing tourists; but the natives here are as much tourists as anyone else. A shop girl on her way home never resists the pleasure of becoming a part of the flow of people moving up and down this wondrous street. Almost every kind of person can be seen strolling here, almost every kind of fashion can be seen in the shop windows. Window shopping is highly cultivated here, the art of window display is practiced with great pain, and the displays change often enough to make a stroll down the Strøget worthwhile at least once a day. This street carries the distinctive flavor of the city itself: quiet, relaxed, private and yet not anonymous, gray but not pale or drab; it is a subtle city almost to the point of being coy. A young English student with a thin beard stands holding hands with his Danish girlfriend as they both study a window advertising the works of some glass blower; an African prince attired in a gray pinstriped double-breasted suit and black leather gloves pushes a baby carriage alongside his blond-haired Danish wife. The city, of course, is chock full of impostors, but there is no necessity on anybody's part to expose such people. Quite to the contrary, the city, the spirit of the city, seems to offer them protection, which is why almost all people here seem as though in exile.

On this particular day it had been raining all morning intermittently, and around one the pale blue sky burst into yellow sunlight. The cobblestone street had been washed clean by the rain and was now a deep red and gave off a strong smell of freshness and earth. People were moving about quickly, the tourists were out with their cameras again, and young, European-style hippies resumed their task of earning a living by drawing Chagalls in the street.

If, in heading toward Kongens Nytorv down the Strøget, one happens to turn right on a certain street, one will find oneself, after some few blocks, face-to-face with a restaurant called the Drop Inn. The Drop Inn is the place you go to meet the "intellectual" bloods. The other place where you can find black people is the Cassanova, which is usually filled with servicemen. One could say that the Drop Inn comes close to being the Big House and Cassanova has the smell of the slave quarters, but, really, such a distinction is misleading because brothers kept a very heavy traffic going from one to the other.

It is three in the afternoon and we find our hero sitting in the Drop Inn hovering over an empty beer mug. He is sitting with some "friends," five in number.

"So you think," Jero said, "they gonna give you some money?"

"The point is," George said, looking up from the mug, "that I *need* some money. *Somebody* is gonna give it to me!"

"It won't be the American embassy," Jero said. He was a very smug, black cat who was supposed to be from Africa. Big deal. And he was a small dude, about the size of a large mouse; in fact, he made you think of a little house mouse all the time you watched him. He didn't like George, he didn't like American Negroes because they were only *half* African; he was under the illusion that he was superior to them because he was *really* from Africa, which got to be a drag.

"Hey man," said Willie, who was from Los Angeles, "you know what, there was a cat who went over to the embassy like that, and they found out that the cat didn't have any bread, so they put his ass out of the country."

"Yeah, I know that's the policy, but I'm not standing for that," George said.

"You know something, Ant," Jero said. George had told them his name was Anthony Miller. He didn't feel he should tell these silly ass mothers what his *real* name was. Like, it's none of their motherhumping business, right? "You know something, Anthony, you're naïve, man. You don't understand that you're living in an International Racist Environment. You don't understand that the white American has a pact with these Scandinavian cats that reads like this: as long as these niggers come over to Copenhagen *with* some American dollars or *earn* some Danish crowns, then they can stay, but when the bread run out, send the niggers back to us; and we'll whip their heads some more and put 'em through some more changes."

"You sure have an accurate view of America," George said.

"You mean them crackers didn't whip your head in the South? You must've licked some white ass if you didn't get your head whip," Jero said.

"You seem to know all the answers, motherfucker," George said.

"Hey, why don't you cats stop arguing all the time," Willie said. "Damn, you get two niggers together for five minutes and they're be cutting each other's throat."

"I didn't ask this cat for his advice," George said.

"No, man, I was just trying to help you out," Jero said. "This cat is so naïve about politics that I felt oblige to say *some*thing."

"Say it to your goddamn *self* then," George said.

"Hey, why don't you cats stop bitching," Willie said.

"Leave the dudes alone," Falstaff said.

"You know what's wrong with this cat," Jero said. "He's evil, motherfucker's evil 'cause he done run outa bread, see. Now, when a nigger runs out of bread he's a evil motherfucker for real."

George looked over at the little black house mouse. He wanted to kick Jero's ass so badly that his foot was trembling. He just wanted to jump up and kick that sad nigger's ass, kick his ass until he was blue in the face, and he wanted to take that little cap he wore on his head and put it into his mouth and then kick his black ass until he ate it. He despised the way the little African was devouring Black American Culture, its vocabulary, its nuances, its soul, and then having the arrogance and nerve to be siddity.

"I don't wanna hear any more of that shit from you," George said.

"Man, I just wanna ask you one more question. How do you expect to get money from the embassy when they don't give *nobody* money? Huh?"

"I might use a gun," George said, "or I might use my cock."

"You think you better than us, huh?" Jero said. "You think you different, huh?"

"Yes," George said.

"How do you think you different from us, man?"

"Motherfucker!!" George leaped up. "Motherfucker, kiss

my ass with your silly paranoiac shit." George walked out the door.

It was around three and he still had time to go to the embassy. He knew he'd have to think up some lie to tell them, knew he had to play some phony role, which finally would not be phony at all since it would get him what he wanted. He was Mr. Jiveass Nigger himself, and knew that there was nothing under the sun that was really phony if it was functional. Being black, being short, being a hopeless homosexual, or being whatever the shit you found yourself being. All that could be functional. Could be useful. Depending on your spirit. Depending on your Energy, Imagination. But cats like Jero didn't relate to that. They related to Bigger Thomas. Yes, Bigger, who went through life living masochistic nightmares, who lived in fear of The Great White Man who in reality was a substitute for some psychic guilt (wanting to fuck their mothers, maybe? or put their black cocks in the asshole of a crew cut?), and not just Negroes but white people also who called it God or President Johnson or the Horror of Death, but Negroes took it harder, took it to mean the Great White Man, and thus spent their lives huddling like wet dogs around the fire and not having enough guts to go out there and see just what it is that's making that noise, yes all those stupid ass Biggers who think violence is sex, who don't have enough cool to seduce a "white" woman but who end up *stealing* a kiss from a "white" girl when he should have fucked her, fucked her so good she would have gotten a glimpse into the immortal soul of the universe and come away from it all a changed woman, fucked her so beautifully that she would come away feeling he was a man, that his fucking (his humanity) had brought out that core of goodness which is in the worst of thieves, that she would come away feeling he was a man, and not a nigger or an animal or an ex-gorilla or something. But no, Bigger's fear was so great that a mere kiss stolen from a white woman's breath (a kiss which should have awakened her from a thousand years' sleep) has to be smothered in a fiery furnace. George Washington could not relate to demoralized Bigger (Nigger Chigger) Thomas. He could relate to Julien Sorel, to Tom Jones; he could relate to the nigger in Malcolm X, LeRoi Jones, James Baldwin, and Eldridge Cleaver. George could relate to the Outcasts of Life and of Literature. He could relate to the protagonists of *The Satyricon* and *The Golden Ass*. But he could not relate to Bigger. He could not relate to stupidity, fear, and demoralization.

When tram no. 2 came, George got on and went to take a seat in the back. He sat down and tried not to look at the beautiful blond girl sitting across from him. Gratuitously, he began thinking about that one spring day him and Reb let the school bus leave them. That was way back in the South and he was in the tenth grade, or was it the eleventh? He thought about it a little longer and it was nice thinking about it. He knew he should have been thinking about the lie and the pose he was going to have to adopt for the people at the embassy, but he was enjoying his reverie, and besides his lies, like a Charlie Parker riff, were more convincing when he did them *à l'improviste*.

When the tram came to his stop, he bopped off in the spirit of a light-spirited bird and began walking down the street toward the embassy. The swinging trees rustling in a shot of unexpected wind, the perfunctory, near-late afternoon sunlight sneaking through the branches, the pure scent of the Copenhagen air that spoke of fresh rain to come—all this made him more conscious of how unusual this visit was going to be.

two

One spring day him and Reb let the school bus leave them.
They walked along the road kicking an old tin can. Then
they went over to Heads and Tails to buy some liquor. They
walked into the living room and George told Head he
wanted a pint. Don't you boys 'spoze to be in school, Tail
said. Tail was Head's twin brother. They were around forty
and had drunk so much rot-gut liquor which they made
themselves that both of them had the reddest eyes you ever
saw. The house was filthy and stinking with dog shit. They
had an old rabbit dog they called Lightnin'. But he was the
laziest ass dog in the county. He had red eyes, too, and was
probably the same age as Head and Tail. Man, what you
talking about school fer, Reb said. Shit, you never went to
school. Hell, I quit school in the first grade, Tail said, laughing. What the fuck you talking about then, Reb said. Head
came back with the pint. George gave him a dollar. That
pint is a dollar and a quarter, Head said. Man, I'll give it to
you sometime. Now come on and gimme my quarter, boy. I
ain't got no mo' money, Head, I swear 'fore God, you kin
search me, George said and held up his arms. Go to hell,
Head said. Reb put the jar to his lips. Gimme a swig of that,
Tail said. Give this fat motherfucker a drink, George said. I
didn't say anything about your mother, did I now, Tail said.
He took the jar from Reb. You better not, I beat the lard
outa your fat ass, George said. You better go beat your old
man, Head said. Ah shet up, nigger, George said. What happened, his old man kicked his ass, Reb said. Stomp a mud-
hole in his ass, Head said. Tail said, shor did. I thought he

was gonna kill that po' boy. Oh, man, he just hit at me and I ducked, George said. You ducked all right, you ducked the wrong way, and man, he was on your little narrow ass like a streak of lightnin' and a bowl of heat. Sheet, George said. Reb was laughing. No, he didn't, did he, Reb said, bent over. These niggers lying, George said. Now why would I lie, huh? Both of us saw it. Ole George was coming around the end of the field with that fast-back mule, which one is that, Georgie boy, you know, and old Willie said now I told that boy to be careful with that drag and old George was whipping the mule with the lines but he didn't know Willie was watching him, and he came flying around that curve and the drag went one way and 'bacco went another and Willie went to Georgie boy's ass. Man, he turned that nigger's ass every way but loose. Reb was down on his knees, laughing. The jar was in Head's hand. George reached over and got it. Sheet, he said. Now, didn't he kick yo' ass, Georgie boy? Now, didn't he? Come on, tell the truth, ain't no sense in lying, now wasn't yo' old man kicking yo' ass down that 'bacco patch like he was driving a tractor, Head was saying. Sheet, George said. He took a swig, a great big one, and began to chuckle to himself. Reb was slapping his hand on his knees, breaking up. Oh man, git the shit up off that flo' 'fore I kick *your* ass. He kicked that po' boy's ass so bad that he ruined a whole half acre of 'bacco, Tail said. A whole half acre of 'bacco, Reb howled from the floor, not a whole half acre, not *that* much! It was almost a acre, Head said, and they all burst out laughing. George had to laugh a little bit himself. Head took the jar and took a swig. Man, get up from that flo', 'fore I start talking 'bout yo' old chicken-eating pappy, George said. Reb got up from the floor, brushing off his pants. Lookit there, got dog shit all over 'im, George said. Where, man, where, Reb said. Oh, that nigger just lying, he mad 'cause his old man kicked his ass in front of everybody, Head said, laughing. Reb started to fold up on the floor again. Sheet, George said, you niggers done drink up all my liquor. Gimme a drink, Reb said. Give you shit, nigger, George said, and took a swig big enough to finish it, but there was still a corner left, so he hand it over to Reb. Niggers drink up all the liquor, Reb said, licking his lips. Hey, Head, I want you to give me back a quarter, George said. Fer what? Fer what? Fer drinking up my liquor. That's what! Your liquor, Head said, hell I just drink the part you didn't pay for. Shit, I paid for all of it, George said. Hey, look you niggers ain't gonna start that shit in my house, Tail said. Man, you call this shit-hole a house, Reb said, with dog shit all over the place and chinches walking around in broad daylight. Git the shit out of 'er, Head said. C'm on let's go. George said, you some crazy motherfuckers, selling people liquor and then heping them drink it up. C'm on let's go, Reb.

They walked out the alley, and Reb asked George what he wanted to do and George said he wanted to go somewhere and read and Reb said shit man that's all you ever think about is reading. Then George said, shit he didn't care what they did. You wanna hitch down to Armour, Reb said. George said O.K. They went out to the highway and caught a ride with a young cracker in a '55 Ford.

Where you boys going, the cracker said.

Just down the road a piece. We'll tell you where, Reb said.

My name is Richard, the cracker said, what's yours.

My name is Byron, George said, and this here is Shelley.

Reb looked over at George, surprised.

Them's some mighty strange names, the cracker said.

We come from up North, George said, we just come down here to visit wit our relatives.

You did, that's very inneresting. I use to live in New York City, the cracker said.

That's where we from, George said, from Harlem.

Well, I'll be, I been to Harlem, once.

It's a very inneresting city, George said, looking out the window. He felt Reb's leg putting pressure on his.

Is that so, the cracker said, glancing over at the boys.

It's a inneresting city, but we rather live in the South, 'cause in the South you kin always get something to eat, see. But sometimes in Harlem you kin go for weeks without a mouthful to eat. I had a brother who went up North, I mean to say, we wuz already living up there and my brother starved to death because he couldn't get no food.

Is that so, the cracker said, you sho' can always get enough to eat down in the South, can't you. There is some colored folks we use to have to feed. We use to live in Bladen County then. Then we move to Wilmington in the city and there ain't no colored around, so my grandmother she goes all the way over across town sometimes to give food to some colored people who used to work for us on the farm back in Bladen County. At first they say they don't want our food, but then they start to coming to they senses and now we git along right nicely.

I know they really appreciate that food, George said, there's a lot of people in the North, like the white people, who have a heart.

Is that so, the cracker said, let me ask you boys something. Y'all had any breakfast?

Breakfast? George said. We ain't have no breakfast in a long time.

Y'all wanna stop and git some?

We as hungry as we can be, but . . .

But what, the cracker said, looking over at George.

We just don't think it right to be eating with white people, George said, we don't wanna eat with white people and we don't want nobody forcing us to. Not even white people.

The cracker didn't say anything. Just stared at the road.

Y'all don't wanna eat with white people, huh, he said.

No, we don't think it's right, George said.

Y'all don't think it's right, huh, the cracker said.

No, we don't think it's any more right for colored to be eating with white people, George said, any more than it's right for white people to be eating with colored people.

I swear, you boys the funniest Northern colored boys I ever met, the cracker said, tell you what I'm gonna do—

At that point George looked out the window, out past the railroad track, and saw his father and mother and the hired hands hoeing in the field. He could tell by the color of the clothes which speck was his mother and which was his father. Dumb motherfuckers always digging in the dirt. Like animals. Niggers always working in the soil like woodchucks.

—tell you what I'm gonna do. 'Fore I let you boys off, I'm gonna give you some money so you kin get a decent meal. And when you go back up North, up there in—

Harlem, George said.

—When you get up there in Harlem, you kin tell them colored people they better come back down here and get something to eat.

I shor will tell 'em, George said, I think I'm gonna be a writer one day and if'n I do, well, I'll just write a book about it; the name of the book'll be called, All the Starving Colored People of the North, Come Home to the South, Supper's on the Table.

Ha, ha, ha, the young cracker laughed, you shor is a smart rastle, ain't you.

What's yo' name, George said, I'll put it on the first page of the book.

My name is Jim Morgan, I got a middle name too. You better use that, 'cause they maybe some other Jim Morgans around, though maybe not in these parts, and it's Melvin. Kin you remember all that?

Let me write it down, George said. He got out a pencil and scribbled in his notebook: Jim Dumbass Cracker Morgan.

You kidding about that book?

No, I ain't kidding, you'll see.

The cracker chuckled.

We gonna get off at the next road, Reb said weakly.

We really appreciate the money, George said.

I ain't give it you, yet, the cracker said, obviously pleased with himself. The car pulled to the side of the road, and the cracker took out two dollars from his pocket.

You boys buy some food with this money, and don't fergit me.

We won't ever fergit you, and when we get back to Harlem, I'll tell everybody about you.

Ha, ha, ha, the cracker said. He had yellow hair and a large, knife-like Adam's apple. They slammed the door and the car drove off.

Goddamnit, Reb said, why'd you tell all them lies.

Shit, how'didya think we got this money? He wouldn't give us shit if'n he knowed we're from here.

But you just start lying *before* that, you were just lying for the fun of it.

Oh, I don't know, George said, it just comes natural with me. I jive people if I don't trust them, see. I jive that motherfucker because I don't feel right with him, you dig my meaning. That white cracker ain't no friend of mine, so I jive him.

And where you get them names, what was it you call me?

I call you Shelley and me Byron. They're poets, man. They were friends, though, because they were into two different things, see. They were rivals.

What's that.

Rivals, you know. They were always doing battle on each other if they met in the street. They're dead now, though.

They white?

Yeah, George said. They crossed the highway and were now walking into the woods.

Why you wanna call me white, man?

I just said that, man, I mean Byron was just like me, man, he was a jive too. And you serious just like Shelley, see.

What you mean by jive, man, you mean he told lies like you?

Reb, everything is a lie. Life is a lie. But people don't know that, see. Only smart people like me know that.

You jiveass nigger, Reb said, laughing.

No, I'm telling the truth.

You jiveass nigger, get away from here.

Well, shit I guess you right, Reb. I am jiving because jiving is the truth, and I'm the living truth.

You the living shit if you don't give me my dollar.

Let's get some wine with it.

No, man, I wanna grease with mine.

What you mean "mine," shit, you ain't got none unless I decide to give you some out of the benevolence of my heart.

What does that mean, Reb asked.

It means the same thing as goodness.

Bee-nevo-LENSE, like that, Reb said.

No, it's Be-NEV-olence, the accent is on the second syllable.

Be-NEV-olence, Reb repeated over and over quietly to himself.

George knew Reb was going to use the word as soon as he got an audience, just to show off. George didn't care. Reb was his main man. They followed the woods around until they could see the high school from between the trees. They sneaked across the road over to the candy store and got some potato chips, two poor boys, and two Pepsis. They had fifty cents left and they went behind the shop and bought a gallon of wine from Jabbo's Uncle Mose. By the time it was three o'clock, they were high off the wine. They went out to catch the school bus back home. They got to the bus, but Buddy Boy who was driving wouldn't open the door. Don't let 'em in, Flossie Belle was shouting from the back window, they didn't go to school t'day, and they half drunk too.

Shit, Reb said, you motherfuckers better open up this here door before I kick your ass out of the benevolence of my heart.

three

He had almost walked past the U.S. Embassy before he realized it; he had expected something tall, with stories stacked
on top of each other, like scoops of ice cream that went a
mile up. No, what he looked at now was less awesome, more
like a granite eagle with spread wings. He was about to
question himself whether this thing was really the embassy
or not, when, as if in answer to his doubt, two MP's strolled
by in perfect time and step, like lovers walking their afternoon walk, hand in hand. He remembered someone telling
him that the American embassy in Copenhagen was the only
embassy that has MP's. (But, after all, he himself was a soldier.) He went in through the glass door and entered what
looked like an indoor garden; in a quick glance, he noticed a
couple darkly dressed, anonymous young men and a very
attractive Danish woman (actually she could have been
some American wife of somebody from Minnesota in Danish
shoes). He turned to his left, having decided that the
woman at the desk in the distance was something of a
receptionist. There was a semicircle of chairs around the receptionist desk, two of which were being occupied by what
could have well been an elderly American couple who had
lost not one but both passports and who were in the process
of begging the embassy to give them substitutes. His ass
dived for a chair opposite the couple and was up again, like
a fast-flying bird dip-fishing. No, he would not sit down and
wait for her to call him; his business was more important
than that, or at least he had to make it appear that way.

"May I help you," said the receptionist, a peroxide blonde;

the stare in her eye placed her from the South or Midwest of the United States, a stare that wondered what this colored person wanted in the American embassy, a stare that greets a black boy selling seeds door to door and who forgets and knocks on some white folks' door, a stare that turned the kindest and most sincere-sounding "May I help you" into the harsh, vicious "What do you want," the answer to which is always "Your life, bitch!"

"I wish to speak to the consul," George said, in a clear, overloud voice. He could take his problem to no one less than the consul, although at first the idea of asking for the consul was frightening; but with important people, audacity is the only policy. So: "I want to speak to the consul" was to be his opening line.

"May I ask why you want to see the consul," she said with stilted politeness. Open-mouthed, the American couple were taking into their weak systems the few words George had exchanged with the receptionist. One of the dark, anonymous young men had also drifted within shore distance and was straining his ears like an animated periscope.

"For personal reasons, I want to see the consul for personal reasons," George said loudly. "Would you tell the consul that I am here," George said with such conviction that he startled *himself*.

"You can't see the consul now; the consul is extremely busy."

"What is it, Miss Claybrooks? Can I help you?" George looked up and saw a middle-aged woman wrapped in a dark gray suit from under which exuded white ruffles. She had some papers in her left hand.

"I'm sorry, Miss Smith, but there is someone who insists

upon speaking with you; I was going to send him to Mr. Bodly."

"Well," Miss Smith said, looking George up and down quickly, "I'll see him; would you come into my office?"

"I'm sorry," the receptionist says, as he went past her; there was the self-righteous glare of the incorrigible Southerner in her gray eyes.

George smiled. He can dig it.

He followed the gray suit through sixty-three seconds of carpeted floors and glass walls, until, finally, he was in a large room surrounded by four walls of books; he caught the title of something called *Congressional Report, 1951,* before sitting down in front of the huge ebony desk, which had a green felt top like a pool table. The woman threw her arms across the green table and her hands began to rip open a pack of Camels.

"You are American, of course," she said, her eyes blinking uneasily; they were light blue and seemed to have something of cold steel in them; yet there was softness in them.

"Yes, from New York."

"How long have you been here?"

"About three months."

"And what are you doing here?"

"Just, just, living . . . spending all my money . . . writing a few lines of verse," George said, lying about the verse, which he couldn't write, although he hadn't tried.

"How'd you get here—boat?"

"No, charter flight from Princeton."

"Oh, you're a student?"

"No, I graduated in June."

"Where did you graduate from?"

"Well, Princeton."

"Princeton!" she exclaimed, and for a moment he thought she was going to go into one of those my-nephew-went-to-Princeton or do-you-know-so-and-so bits, but her sudden enthusiasm was to lead to other equally notorious clichés:

"Graduating from Princeton, and loafing around in Copenhagen, how do you explain that; you should be back home helping out others"—George knew she was trying to say he should be joining Martin Luther King—"you went to Princeton, got a good education, I didn't even finish high school, I only went to the eleventh grade, but I was lucky, times have changed, of course; but you certainly should put that education of yours to some use—"

"Well, I plan to," said George, somewhat taken back at the frontal attack, which, though identifying the woman as some variety of American liberal, offered him a bit of encouragement.

"With a degree from Princeton, you shouldn't be caught without money," she said, in a confidential tone. How do you defend yourself against that? She was going to reprimand him, befriend him (to an extent), then give him the four hundred crowns, and make him promise never to do it again. So he would have to sit there and take it.

The softness in the eyes resulted from a peculiar style of blinking, a blink that could easily be taken as a wink, a blink that softened the cold stare of her blue eyes.

"We need more colored leaders like Martin Luther King," she said suddenly, as though George's pecuniary situation and the civil-rights struggle in America were all part of the same question. "I wish to God your people would listen to him, and we wouldn't have the kind of embarrassing . . . the kind of violence we have now—" she indicated with her hand the headlines in *The New York Times* lying on her desk. George had not read the papers, but he knew there had been a riot recently in Harlem that had spread into other parts of the city.

Unwilling to give his own views, he changed the subject, although it was obvious that the woman was brooding over a problem that had long ago become something personal.

"Are you the consul here; I mean, I guess you are about as surprised to see a Negro with a degree from Princeton as I am to see a woman in the position of consul; as you know, the two most discriminated groups in America are the Negro and women," George said.

"Well, I am the consul; I've just received my official appointment from Washington last week."

"Did you go to diplomacy school," George said, winging it, of course.

"No, I just worked my way up the ladder; I quit school when I was in the eleventh grade"—she said this with pride —"joined the Waves, became the private secretary of a lieutenant general during the war (the Second World War), and after the war they needed someone to send to Africa to act as secretary to the consul in Morocco, and I spent four years there, then I went to Japan, Sweden, and finally here. When the consul became sick and eventually retired—he is back in the States dying now—I was the next person in line for succession."

"Where do you come from in the States?"

"Oklahoma, small town in Oklahoma," she said in a tone of the local-girl-makes-good tradition.

"Oklahoma, had a roommate once from Oklahoma," George lied.

"Where was he from in Oklahoma?"

"I think, Tulsa, yeah Tulsa, he was my roommate for only a little while, didn't get to know him well at all, but it was Tulsa."

"Tulsa's about 150 miles from where we lived."

"You say, 'lived.' Your family still live there?"

"Oh, yes."

"That's nice—" He wanted to tell the woman that he had once heard in Central Park Rodgers and Hammerstein's musical *Oklahoma!* and that it made him feel very fine about Oklahoma.

The consul had gotten lost in her reminiscence and now suddenly jerked herself back into the situation at hand by asking what "the particular nature of his problem" was.

"I want to borrow four hundred crowns from the embassy, which I will repay when my father sends me money in a couple weeks."

"You want to *borrow* four hundred crowns," she laughed, in half disbelief.

"Yes," George said.

"Four hundred crowns," she repeated, saddling her chin mockingly into her hand.

"I figure that's what I need to pay my rent and pay back some friends that I owe, and eat a good meal," he said dryly.

"We have precedents established here for this kind of situation. What we do is offer to send you back home, and have you repay the government when you get back. We never give out cash, not even lend cash, not even to our own staff . . . Did you know our policy?"

"No, I didn't know that, I'm sorry; I don't want to go home. If you can't give me the money, I'd find some other way—" This last statement was supposed to imply some degree of militant imminence—it was a threat, that if they didn't give him the goddamn money, he'd, he'd . . . who knows what he might do; that was a question the answer to which was supposed to loom dangerously, fearfully, in *their* own minds and dreams. Right?

"I am afraid I can't help you." she said, looking at him now with her cold, unblinking eyes. She was playing the cold bitch. She pushed herself back from her desk and, with her head hunched deeply into the shoulder blades like the head of a turtle reclining back into its shell, she said, "I am afraid there is nothing I can do. I have some authority here, but we have policies." She paused, as though to allow the full import of what she had said to soak into the cross-grained texture of his consciousness. He stared at her. She had a very hard, masculine-featured face, thin, cruel, dry lips, no cosmetics (except for the false eyelashes, which were now in disuse), no sign of femininity (except the white ruffs around her throat, which were now smothered in the sharp concave of her hunched shoulders). She wasn't even a liberal, but rather a red-neck from Oklahoma, a red-neck who, through hard work, hustling, and a few strategic affairs with the right man, had made it to what she inevitably thought of as the top; a red-neck cracker!

She threw herself forth with the feigned compromised gesture of a corporation executive, landing her arms on the table in an all-encompassing semicircle. "The only thing I can do is get you a job."

If she wanted to lend him the money, she could do it easily enough. With some hopeless finality, what she wanted was this: she wanted him, despite his degree, to work for the four hundred crowns. The racists' panacea for all the civil-rights problems! He'd play along with her, but somewhere along the line he was going to trip her up.

"What kind of job," he asked.

"Well, let's see. I think one of our political analysts said he needed some help," she said, and rose from the desk. "I'll be right back." Her legs, as she went away from him, were not particularly bad; in fact, they were quite good. She had a fairly well-shaped body, a more than substantial posterior— all of which stood her in good stead in her rise to consul. George felt the heaviness of his semi-erect penis. It was hard as shit. Once at a summer party on Nantucket he had met a beautiful, blond girl from North Carolina who had almost said she was a racist ("Well, I think I have a perfect right not to want to go out with Negro men . . . I just don't find them attractive at all") and who went to Radcliffe; and he got the hardest hard he'd ever remembered having as he stood there in his bathing trunks and a whiskey sour trying to decide whether to engage her in an argument or to throw the damn drink into her face—he eventually did both; whenever he met a Southern woman, he had only to hear her speak in her Southern hue, or make the slightest reference to that blessed place he knew so well, and he would get a hard-on.

The consul brought with her a tall, thin man with a boy's face. "This is our political analyst, Thomas Rowan, and, Tom, this young man here graduated from Princeton University and is now bumming around in Copenhagen, as broke as he can be—" There was something of the liberal in her voice now, which had lost some of its coldness but was not yet friendly; there was also something of the maternal glint in her eyes as she went on: "—he wants to borrow some money until his dad sends him some, but I told him we simply have certain policies here that if we violated, every American tourist would feel justified by stepping in here and asking for the same favor, and we are far from being a bank to American tourists—" George guessed that the political analyst must have had some notorious record of being a liberal too from the extent to which the consul was apologizing; George even suspected the political analyst of being a New York Jew. He certainly looked it. "And so I was telling him—" the consul went on "—that what we may be able to do is to arrange for him to do some work around here, and I just remembered that you said you needed someone, why don't you speak with him and see what you can do—"

"What's your name," Thomas said, extending his hand.

"Paul Winthrop, thank you," George said, clasping the extended hand. He glanced at the consul in a way that told her he knew she had committed another *faux pas* in not having the grace enough to ask him his name.

"What was your major?"

"Literature and philosophy." Lying—naturally.

"Oh, really, mine was too. Philosophy, that is," said Thomas Rowan, very pleased to find some snatch of conversation to hide his uneasiness behind.

"Where did you go?"

"Stanford," Thomas Rowan said. "Well, look, step into my office." And as they walked out, George took malicious pleasure in having excluded the consul from their esoteric conversation. She was still a country bumpkin, still a racist bitch no matter how hard she worked. There was something very dark in her hard, granite face as George walked out the door.

"I understand Stanford is a beautiful place," he said to Thomas Rowan.

"It's a good school, an excellent school," Thomas Rowan

said. "I did graduate work there; I met my wife there and my daughter goes there now."

"What year is she?" The question was too automatic and he felt for a second he had shown himself too interested in this man's daughter. A foolish thought.

"She's a junior, but she's taking this year off and spending it here with me. She wants to be a writer."

"Really, that's something I'd like to do myself, write," George said, almost daring the man to go further.

"Well, maybe I'll get a chance to introduce you to her."

That was further than George was willing to go, and he was about to change the conversation when the door opened, revealing the consul's head.

"Paul," she said, using his name for the first time, "would you like to have dinner with me; a good meal won't hurt you, will it?" And she looked at Thomas Rowan, winked, and gave a little maternal chuckle.

"No, sure that's great," George said. Bitch!

"Have him stop by my office, Mr. Rowan, when you are finished." More smiles for Rowan.

The consul's reaction was one of jealousy; she was afraid Rowan was upstaging her with his liberal role; and no doubt she had some alienation complex about not having a college degree too. If she only knew.

"Well," said Rowan, sitting down in his swivel chair, "I wanted somebody to wash windows, but you won't want to do that kind of thing, would you?"

"No."

"I don't really have anything then; there may be a possibility in my clerking system, but it won't be until next week before I can tell you for sure. Leave your address with me and I will get in touch with you on that."

George scribbled out his address on a piece of paper.

"Well, okay," said Thomas Rowan. "Here, you'd better get on down to Miss Smith's office before you miss a free meal."

They walked back into the consul's office. It had been a useless interview; the whole thing with Rowan was farcical; Rowan knew he didn't have a job for him from the very beginning, but he couldn't resist playing the role of benevolent liberal; yet if George had consented, wouldn't Rowan have given him the job of washing his fucking floors? Did the consul send him down to Rowan knowing that Rowan wanted someone to wash floors? She must have known he would not take such a job, and he doubted that she expected him to. He suspected that she was testing him for something else she had in mind, but what it was he could not guess.

Smiling politely, she said, "Would you like to eat American food or Danish?"

"Danish, of course. American food is too heavy for my empty stomach," he said. She led him out toward the receptionist area, and they stopped in front of a man who looked like Burt Lancaster.

"This is our economic adviser, Mr. Kornblum; and this, Mr. Kornblum is an American friend of mine—" the possessiveness was something new "—a Princeton graduate, stranded in Copenhagen."

There was a brief exchange of greetings. Handshakes. Smiles. One of the young, darkly dressed men opened the back door of an American car, a Lincoln, closed the door, and got in the front behind the wheel.

"Take us to the Coq d'Or on H. C. Andersens Boulevard," Miss Smith said.

four

The driver, a young Dane in his early twenties, peeped through the rear-view mirror with surreptitious curiosity.

"What did Mr. Rowan say?" Miss Smith asked.

"He said he had nothing."

"That's funny, he said he wanted someone to wash windows just a few days ago. You don't mind washing a few windows, do you?"

"No," George lied. "No matter how high you get, you can't get above work, can you? I can say one thing for my daddy; he certainly made me proud of working with my hands." There was a silence and they exchanged significant glances; the oppressive silence remained.

"Yes, I was born and raised on a farm and have great respect for manual labor," George said, muscling up all the irony possible in the tone of his voice.

"I'll see if I can't get you a job tomorrow mixing drinks for a party that's taking place at the embassy tomorrow," she said, taking his irony like a punch to the jaw and, in returning it, hitting him below the belt. "You can mix drinks, can't you?"

"Gin-and-tonic, Manhattans, Bloody Marys . . ." George said, hating the idea of even imagining himself playing nigger bartender to these American representative shitheads and racists.

"That's just fine; most of the embassy people are straight-on-the-rocks types, so you shouldn't have much difficulty."

The black Lincoln shot down Gothersgade, bypassing Kongens Nytorv. Outside the window rough, red faces;

young pallid faces; fineass legs, legs clothed in various gar-
ments; tired eyes, excited eyes; blond hair, brown hair, black
hair cluttered the street corners in obedience to red lights,
while others rode bicycles under the protection of green
ones. It was five o'clock and some of Copenhagen's labor
force was going directly home, but most of it was intent on
filling the bars, jazz clubs, dance halls, Tivoli Garden, movie
houses, bathhouses, rest rooms, and other people's rooms before going home. In his mind's eye, George saw the brothers
at Drop Inn and Cassanova settling in for the night's long
ride. *Dumb motherfuckers.*

"*Hvordan har De det?*" the Danish waitress said, smiling
politely as they entered the restaurant.

"*Tak, godt,*" George said.

"Do you speak Danish?" Miss Smith asked as they sat
down at their table.

"Oh no, not really, just a few words; have to be polite, you
know; do you?"

"God no, that's one of the good things about working for
the embassy here in Denmark—you don't have to be both-
ered with learning the language."

The restaurant was a very expensive one, and its wealth
had a somewhat not unexpected effect on our hero. Inside
his stomach George felt a bit nervous, as though he were
being taken for ice cream by his mother in a fancy *white*
drugstore. The red plush carpet, upholstered chairs, the velvet wallpaper, the elaborate silverware setting (What in the
hell was he supposed to do with *three* forks?) forced quickly
and unobtrusively to George's mind the image of his previous destitute state.

Being one to rapidly adapt to any new environment, however, George immediately gained his balance—so much so

that, had one not been previously acquainted with his true history, upon seeing him conducting Ruth Smith into her chair with the air of self-assurance with which he did, one would have been greatly persuaded that George Washington had been accustomed to this kind of style all his life.

To the left, three tables had been pulled together, and six what must have been wives of American businessmen were chatting along in cracking metallic Midwestern accents. On the right, a man whose shiny head peeped through thin gray hair was hovering over his plate, in intimate conversation with a yellow-haired girl of about nineteen whose reluctant and fidgeting hand was clasped in his. At another table, two very attractive American girls were trying to pretend that they were French. George couldn't make out exactly what was being said, but it had to do with some

"*garçon*"

"*qui est un animal*"

"*mais*"

"*il est très bel, n'est-ce pas?*"

George ordered lobster with cauliflower. The cuisine was obviously among the best in Copenhagen; yet Miss Smith was somewhat uncomfortable throughout the ordeal; and it was his impression that the source of this uneasiness was simply that they were basically incompatible, yet for some strange reason she seemed determined to tolerate him. After they had consumed half a bottle of French wine, however, their talk began to loosen up.

"Do you have a girlfriend here in Copenhagen?" Miss Smith asked at one point. And at another, "My close friends call me Ruth, so why don't you do the same."

"Okay," he said smilingly. It occurred to him, for a moment, that he should make some advances, for the sake of establishing some amorous rapport with the woman who could very well be his salvation. As she got drunker, a different woman, a softer person, emerged. How old was she? Around forty? What would it be like making love to this bitch? Does she have a lover? What kind of lover would she have? Some old fathead motherfucker. Down in her lap her skirt had pulled halfway up her thigh, and his dick tightened. No, she wouldn't think of sleeping with me. Shit, maybe that cracker would. He began to take her clothes off and lay them on the table. Look at that bitch's pink bikini panties.

"Oh, hello, Miss Smith," a girl said. "I thought that was you, but I wasn't sure." The girl glanced over at George. "You're American, aren't you?" she said, showing a beautiful set of teeth made whiter by a heavy suntan. French Riviera, no doubt.

"This is Mr. Rowan's daughter, Paul," Miss Smith said.

"Hi, I met your father at the embassy," George said, standing and taking her hand.

"Are you working at the embassy?"

"No."

"What *do* you do?"

"Well, nothing. I write a little poetry."

"Oh, good. My name is Gloria, what's yours?"

"Paul," George said.

"May I have a check," Miss Smith said to the waiter.

"Are you leaving?" asked Gloria.

"I'm afraid so, I have to get up early tomorrow," Miss Smith said, and turning to George, "I can drive you home if you'd like."

"Well . . . uh . . . actually I have to go somewhere else and see a friend; it's not far from here, but thanks anyway."

"Just so you don't forget, I'd like to speak to you for a few seconds before I leave," she said, and turning to Gloria, "I'll send him right back."

"Well, it was nice meeting you," Gloria said.

When they were outside, Miss Smith turned to him. "Call me tomorrow, and why don't you give me your address and the telephone there. I'll be certain to get you something to do by tomorrow."

He scribbled out his address, and was about to say good night, when Miss Smith handed him an envelope.

"That's my number at home," she said. When she took his hand, she gave it a delightful squeeze. As the car pulled away, he turned and looked at the folded paper. As he unfolded it, some Danish currency sailed out. He picked it up. It was 100 kroner.

five

His original intention was to return to the Coq d'Or and try to fuck Gloria, but the 100 kroner sent him in a different direction.

When he reached the Drop Inn, he realized that he was completely out of breath; he was panting and he was feeling very excited. He dashed into the joint.

The poet Ned Green was pontificating to a small group of people who had surrounded him. Ned was a poet, a black American poet, born, as the biographical sketch on the back of his thin book of verse, called *All of Ned and No More*, had it, in Mississippi in 1921. Long before he had ever met Ned, long before he himself had even come to Europe, George had discovered the volume, *All of Ned and No More*, in a raggedy bookstore in the Village, and had read it with great interest; Green was, like a rocket out of its resting pad, out of the beat-poetry era; beat was very important to his poetry; he had heard Green read once, and Green had succeeded in making his voice sound like an ax riffing, then like a trumpet blaring.

The first time he met Green in Europe was when he was walking down a street in Copenhagen with a beautiful Norwegian girl whom he had known a little less than an hour. Suddenly the girl let out a scream, which led George to believe that the young woman, like the hero of some Bergman film, had just seen death; she only said, pointing in a faint way to a black figure passing into the shadow of another street, "There goes Ned Green." George and the girl had turned to go and find this Ned Green, although George had to insist upon doing so against the girl's will. When he saw Ned's face, the full, round beard, the hairline that receded back into the baldness of his head, he knew this was the Ned Green on the front of the thin book of beat poetry he had read some long time ago back in New York. He told the poet he had read his book, and the poet was very pleased, more pleased than one would think a poet should be about a thin volume of verse that's interesting but not that great.

A week later, when they were sitting in a restaurant without the girl, George told Ned about how the girl had screamed when she saw him on the street that day. George had gone to bed with the girl three times. Maybe Ned would talk about how good her snatch was. But he surprised George by not saying anything like that. He thought the poet might say something like that; he had heard that the poet was married to an African woman and had children by her, and he had read in an anthology of black poetry that he was married to a woman in Detroit and had two or three children by her, so he thought the poet was a cold-hearted lady's man. But when Ned said that the girl was a very nice kid, George was a little surprised.

"I met her in Paris, and I told her I had to go to Morocco, but she wanted to come along, so she came and we slept out in the open in sleeping bags and hitched during the day. Then one morning I saw she was sick or something, and then she tells me she's in love with me, jack. I make her go right back to Paris. I hadn't seen her since, until I ran into her with you." When George had said to the girl that there must have been something between her and this poet Ned in order for her to scream so upon just seeing him, she said there was nothing, she'd just met him in Paris.

Now George walked into the Drop Inn. Ned saw him.

"Hey, man, what's happenin'," Ned said.

"Hey, man, how's Paris," George said, coming over.

"Hot, man, hot. It was a very heavy and beautiful scene," Ned informed him. "I just got back from a reading with Langston Hughes."

George found a chair, and Ned went on about the poetry reading, about how black it was. George was introduced to one of the poets who had come to Copenhagen to escape the heat of Paris; he shook hands with a very skinny, dark Negro girl who, from just looking at, one would not think she knew much about poetry of any kind; she was with an equally skinny and unattractive Danish boy. There were a couple of Danish girls in the group and a few American males (i.e., Doc, Billy, the ass-man Leopard).

One of the Danish girls, pointing to Ned's African skull-cap, said, "Why do you guys wear those funny little hats?"

"Funny little hats," Ned repeated with disdain, "what the fuck do you mean 'funny little hats.' Why do Danish men wear the shit on their heads that they do, you don't call *that* funny, do you? Why do the French and the Americans wear the shit they wear? Goddamnit, people have been wearing hats since the beginning of time, the cave men wore things on their heads, and nobody ever said a damn thing; but as soon as a black man starts wearing something that's representative of his culture, his blackness, you want to know—" and here he began to imitate the loose and heavy accents of the Danish girl, who had turned red with chagrin, as everybody else was nearly in tears with laughter "—suddenly you want to know, 'why d'you wear those funny little hats?' "

George burst into laughter, for he knew, as did everyone

else who knew Ned, that the girl had gotten herself into something from which she was not going to extricate herself easily.

Ned turned to the girl with a half-smiling, half-serious look on his lips. He took off his hat and held it like a bird in his hand, and put it in smelling distance of the girl's nose.

"Now tell me, what's so funny about this piece of cloth? Why is this a funny little thing to you?" Everybody, except the girl, began to laugh. "No, this ain't no laughing matter," Ned protested. "I'm serious as I can be. I want you to tell me why you call this 'a funny-looking thing,' because maybe you know something I don't and I wanna know it too."

"Oh, let up off her," Doc said, "she's not hip to Blackness."

"No, no, I can't let up off her," Ned said, "she got to be educated too. If there is anyone who will listen to black people, it's the white woman; we gotta hit the weakest link in the chain, jack; no, man, I can't let up off her, that's why we have the situation in America today; it's the white woman, man; we gotta get to that bitch and straighten out her mind, man. You take in the South, in the deep South, you know why there's all these lynchings, man? Because these white broads down South don't fuck, they don't fuck anybody, not to mention their husbands! A white cat gets married and his old lady doesn't fuck, she 'makes love' and so he thinks she is fucking somebody else, he goes out and strings up some niggers, thinking the niggers are getting it, and the niggers think the ofay boys is getting it, but the truth of the matter is, man, that ain't nobody getting it, unless it's the psychiatrist, because the bitch ain't got nothing to give; her mind, her soul has been washed out with Miss Clairol, with Yardley, and store-bought beauty; and Sapphire ain't no better, she's worse, she goes around imitating Miss Ann, imitating that dead, dry bitch, so, man, I tell you I can't let up off this fine Danish lady, 'cause I got to teach her something." He reached out and laid his hand seductively on the girl's arm.

"I think black is very beautiful," the Danish girl volunteered, offering her opinion up to the bloody altar, like some vestal virgin.

"Honey," coaxed Ned (now in the seducer's voice), "that's what we got to teach the world, and we can't do it by calling my hat 'a funny-looking thing.' My hat is just like anybody else's hat, it's just a hat I put on my head; there are French hats, English hats, Danish hats, Norwegian hats, Dutch hats, American hats, Chinese hats, Vietnamese hats, and this one here on my noggin is an African hat; but that don't make no difference—" he could have been talking to a child now "—it's still just a little old hat, and not a 'funny little thing.'"

George got up and ordered some beer, and sat down at a table with Doc, who was sitting off from the crowd that was around Ned. Doc was something of a tragic figure behind a clown's mask. George respected him very much. Doc (Melvin Jerrell was his real name) had gotten his medical degree from Harvard, came from a distinguished Negro family (his father and grandfather were dentist and drugstore owner, respectively) in St. Louis, and possessed a hue of dull pessimism about his person, his movements, which led one to believe that his reasons for not taking up root in the American soil were more real than those of the rest of the American blacks who found shelter in the Drop Inn from the bombardments of American influence.

Doc said once that although they (black expatriates) had (some of them unconsciously) escaped to Copenhagen from America, the irony of the situation was that in Copenhagen one found America in its purest, most irreducible form; and

another time he had said that (George was at the time saying that the reason he came to Scandinavia was to get the
White Bitch out of his system by wallowing in Whiteness
until he could live without it) blacks could not deal with the
white problem in Europe because the Europeans, the Scan-
dinavians, weren't white.

In all, Doc had said some pretty profound things, and
George had decided that there was more to Doc than the
weird tales he told about his misadventures with strange
women. There was something beneath the surface, something very real that kept Doc from America, and the superfi-
cial thing of race conflict had little or nothing to do with it;
and even when Doc talked about his women, about the
tricks they pulled on him, and the tricks he pulled on them,
these things had nothing whatsoever to do with Doc the
man; even when they got off into literature, a subject which
they both enjoyed, there was nothing in it that had to do
with Doc; Doc was somewhere else, he was off contemplat-
ing the darkness of an abyss that gaped like an open grave;
one was so certain that this was what Doc might have been
doing that one was afraid to ask him, afraid that Doc might
say yes, it's true, afraid that Doc might tell one what he
saw.

Yet, Doc had a comedian's face; the ends of his lips were
permanently turned up, the skin around his eyes eternally
squinched, his eyes forever laughing—his face was a mask—
not a momentary expression; and what was behind this mask
was what is always behind a mask—another mask, although
this one was closer to the core, the unmaskable thing.

"Ned's right," Doc was saying. "The White Man is going
to die a death of repression. The Great Father of Repression

is gonna be his own victim." George sucked at his beer and gave Doc an attentive glance.

"The White Boy has passed Death, Sin, Trickery, Disease, Filth, but mostly Death, off on the nigger—that's what being a nigger means: that you have to appease Death at an early age, so that the white boys can live longer; and white people think that as long as they can keep the niggers from living next door, from fucking their daughters, they can keep Death out of their lives—man, when you see these racist bastards killing blacks in the street, you can believe they think they're fighting Death."

"Yeah, that's right," George said. "But this shit just didn't start yesterday; the nigger existed a helluva long time in the psyche, the literature of the Western head, long before they got to Africa. Did you ever read *Comus*, by Milton?"

"No," Doc said, hunching forward.

"If you read it right, if you are able to see that the whole thing is really about the nigger marrying Miss Ann all over again, the thing is very contemporary. What it pretends to be is a dialogue between a virgin, the Lady, as Milton calls her, and Comus, who represents the unconscious sex urge, the magician, the son of Circe, and—get this—Comus lives in a black forest, you know, the precursor to the ghetto. The Lady has to go through that forest—I mean, she's got to get in there and dig some sex or at least have a good excuse for not indulging—in order to arrive at her destiny—a well-lighted garden. Her two brothers—like every white boy—are waiting for her, but fear she will run into Comus—which she does. The elder brothers think they have nothing to worry about because their sister is protected with Chastity."

"That's why she's repressed," Doc added.

"—Yeah, but the other brother makes it clear that this cat Comus is a bitch, you know the cat's a witch doctor, he changes his appearance and shit like this. For Comus, God is Man; and what Man does, be it fuck virgins or whatever, is Godly. Finally Comus gets tired of the Lady's phony philosophical rationales, and works some magic shit on her. At the very same time the brothers break in on the scene—"

"The lynching is on—" Doc said, laughing.

"—Yeah, they hit the nigger across the head and shit like that, but a good Spirit—Norman Mailer all over again—comes along and hips them to the fact that although they have physically conquered Comus, they have not released the Lady from his magical powers. You know, you can't fight magic with shotguns. Yet the source of Comus's magic is centered in his 'Rod,' that's what Milton called it, and I take the cat literally! The Spirit tells them that they blew the thing, that they should have gotten hold of his Rod—"

"His Dick," said Doc.

"—Yeah, so they have to go get another spirit, Sabrina, to undo this Black Magic; but this second spirit is a fantasy of the White Boys' because there ain't no power strong enough in the world to undo Black Magic."

"Psychoanalysis," answered Doc.

"No, baby, psychoanalysis *is* Black Magic," George said.

"Oh, yeah," Doc conceded. He frowned contemplatively for a moment, and added, "And Death, too."

"You want another beer?" George said, getting up from the table.

"Get me an Elephant," Doc said.

six

After three hours of drinking Elephant beer, George and Doc made their way, as they often did, to Café Royale, by way of Cassanova. Cassanova sat squatted in the darkest shadows in the middle of a street, which, due to the great number of black American soldiers and young Danish girls who used the street, had gained the notoriety of being a back street. If the Drop Inn was the purgatory, Cassanova was the inferno where all was burnt into the blackest char, where all were doomed; doomed were the young Danish girls, who were not prostitutes (unless you came on like you were white, nigger!) but who had the prostitute's vision, the prostitute's eyes, the prostitute's walk.

As they came up the street, a group of blacks were spewing out of the mouth of the joint. A white man, a Dane, was crossing over to the other side of the street.

"Hey, motherfucker," one of the soldiers was shouting to the man. The other soldiers laughed. The old man tried not to run, yet he could not make himself walk. A hand slapped a khaki-clothed leg, "AAAHH, let's get that motherfucker." The soldiers laughed.

"They're just bull-shittin'," George said, mostly to himself.

He and Doc were coming toward the old man, who, when he discovered them, began to shake visibly and started to turn and run back into the arms of the soldiers.

"We're not gonna kick your ass," George yelled out to him. The old man came toward them, timidly; then George smiled, to encourage him. *"God nat,"* George let out as he passed him.

"They ought've kicked his ass," Doc said. "Kill his ass."
George looked at Doc. Could he have meant that? Wasn't
Doc too profound for that kind of pettiness? Wasn't he beyond the tired categories of black and white? Wasn't he an
artist, a tragic and doomed man, doomed because he had no
choice but to live with the realization that life is meaningless? And wasn't this realization the thing that tied him to
Doc? He looked at Doc's face. The man had a young face,
brown as a walnut, a face that had grown old too soon.
What kind of man lived behind that face?

There was a time when George thought he might tell Doc
his real name, and would not feel he had to continue lying
about who he really was. He actually felt an affinity to the
man's weirdness, thought that Doc understood the profound
necessity behind lying and pretending. He was once certain
that it would be Doc who would be the first to know. Yes,
Doc would understand about names. But when Doc had
yelled at the scared old man, something tightened in
George, tightened up so inside him that he trembled with
fright. Why had he said that? Why? Goddamnit, why?

They walked into the place. A sergeant with his hat on the
table was sitting with a big blonde on his knee, teasing her
with his American jokes; on the right and left, black soldiers
were rapping, touching, caressing, biting, coaxing, threaten-
ing beautiful, sometimes not so beautiful, young and sometimes not so young, women. Some of the women were Swedish, and came over with the speedboat from Malmö with the
single-minded purpose of spending the weekend in Cassanova and the hotel rooms about Cassanova.

Cassanova was also the only place in Copenhagen where
Soul Music could be heard; the Danish girls learned from
the black soldiers how to do the Monkey, the Boogalou, the

Twist. And if you were walking along a street (say, near the king's palace) and heard from the nurses' quarter of a hospital James Brown bellowing out, "Papa's got a Brand New Bag," you knew that someone up there is a "Cassanova girl."

Doc and George sat down, drinking from two mugs as they listened to Otis Redding. A black soldier came up and asked them if they were in the service and after they answered he then went on to say that he was never going to return to the States. He got Doc's and George's support. After half an hour with the soldier, George was getting bored.

Across from them another black soldier was telling his Danish girl a joke about a colored man. This colored man was in a multitude of people following Jesus across the desert, and they had been walking all morning and then when the sun was straight up (meaning it was lunchtime), Jesus turned to the multitude and said: Gather ye unto ye a rock. So everybody got a medium-size rock, everybody except this colored dude; he got the tiniest pebble he could find. It was so small that he could hide it in the wrinkle in the palm of his hand. The reason he got such a little rock is, hell he figured they were going to have to carry the damn things and he didn't wanna be lugging all that dead weight.

But no, Jesus had another purpose in mind; he turned to the multitude and spoke these words: The rocks ye hold shall be turned to bread, so that ye may eat! Suddenly all the rocks were transformed into bread, and everybody had a fairly nice loaf because everybody had got a fairly normal-size rock. Everybody, that is, except this colored man. He had in the palm of his hand the tiniest crumb you ever seen in your life; I mean, it was just about the size of his pebble, and when he went to put it in his mouth he missed and dropped it in the sand, where, because the grains of sand was larger than the crumb, he lost it. Man, this dude was so mad with Jesus Christ that it was all he could do not to go up side Christ's head. And he was hungry. He was afraid to go over to Christ and tell him what happened—I mean, you know everybody's always accusing us colored people of shucking and jiving, so I mean, he didn't even have a chance. So he just went on holding his grudge.

Then around when the sun began to limp into sand (around dinnertime), Christ turned once again to the multitude and spoke thusly: Gather unto ye a rock. Three other black soldiers' ears had turned homewardly and were already cracking up behind the joke, the way the brother was telling it: taking his time, thoroughly enjoying his rap. And they were way ahead of the Danish girls who listened through rubber ears. Gather unto ya a rock. Man, when the brother heard this he broke for the biggest rock he could find, which was about ten feet tall and musta weighed five or six tons; he couldn't lift it, so he threw his arms around it and cried out: I got mines, Lord! And then the Lord turned and saw the huge rock and then he threw his finger out at the rock and say: Verily, verily, I say unto you, *upon this rock I shall build my church.* Then the brother said: The hell you is. You gonna make some bread outa this rock, now ain't you, Lord . . . I mean, I didn't get none the last time . . .

The brothers who had gathered around the table burst out laughing. Of course, it was an old one, but that only made it better. One of the brothers in uniform said y'all know the one about Efan the Bad Nigger and then he said during slavery times every plantation had a bad nigger, and the slave masters would be beefing about who had the baddest nigger, and so this particular slave master named Brian Coker had what he actually thought was the baddest nigger in the South. The nigger's name was something like Kocomo, was about ten feet tall, had muscles like a mule and the general appearance of an ex-gorilla. Now the other slave master he had a nigger named Efan who used to go around bragging to his master and the other slaves or anybody he came in contact with about how bad he was. He was nothin' but a skinny, puny little-bitty fellow, but if you listen to him wolf about himself you'd think he was really bad. He was nothin' but a bullshit artist, see.

Another brother sat down at the table with a beer. He was round like a big, black rubber ball. He turned the chair backwards, straddled it, and threw his head back, laughing. He was wearing a red shirt with huge green and white palm leaves spread over it, and a pair of tan short pants. He said, What did you say that other bad nigger was, an ex-gorilla? Then he howled with laughter. Everybody else, the girls included, laughed too. Yeh, someone said, an ex-gorilla. He sho' musta been bad. Hey, man, go on with the story, some G.I. in uniform said. Anyway, the red-haired storyteller continued, this jiveass called Efan had his master going around thinking he was really bad, and so the master told Brian Coker the owner of that ex-gorilla that . . . The brother who came on like a big black rubber ball was bouncing on the floor . . . told him that he'd bet his plantations that Efan could beat his bad nigger. So the bet was on, 'cause Coker knew his nigger was really bad. They set the date, the place and time, and took care of all the formalities. Then the master went home and took Efan aside, and said, Efan, I have great confidence in you, I have just placed the destiny of not only the life and livelihood of my own family, but also that of your own people, in your hands. You're the baddest nigger in this section of the country, as you yourself have so many times stated, and so I have made it possible for you to use your talent, use it to further the cause of your people. If you beat Brian Coker's nigger next Monday, then we will win a whole plantation, and you'll be set up as overseer. I know you can do it, Efan. Do it for me, and more important —*do it for your people!!* Now, all the while the master was talking this way, Efan was shaking inside because he knew that his mouth had written a check his ass couldn't cash. He was scared but he didn't want the master to know it. He didn't want his master to think he wasn't as bad as he said he was. Efan had a lotta pride. And it was impossible for him to ever go back on his word, even though that *word* was straight from the mouth of Mr. Jiveass Nigger himself. Efan was a man who always backed up his bullshit with action, which explains why he was always getting himself in these impossible situations. So when the master said, I know you will skin the nigger alive, Efan, my man, when he said this, Efan said, Boss, go out there and dig a grave. What for, the master said. Efan said, 'Cause I'm gonna kill him, boss. Wait a minute, boss, you don't have to build no large grave, just a small hole like this. And he made a hole with his two open hands. Just a small hole what you use to bury guts in to keep 'em from the dogs will do, 'cause I'm going crumble that nigger into little bits, I'm gonna pack him into a bucket, boss, like he was dirt. Man, if that master only knew that this skinny nigger was lying!

So for the next five days Efan lived like a king. He had the master working for him. Every morning he'd tell the boss, Boss, you go saddle up your best saddle horse you got there. I'll be down as soon as I take a bath, shave, and get my shoes shined. Hitch the horse out there, comb the mane,

and get them brand-new trace chains out. Efan told master
if he was gonna beat the nigger he had to eat well, and so he
ate six meals a day in the Big House with Miss Ann and the
white folks. He wore a white suit, a red handkerchief around
his neck, got a haircut, had one of the slaves cleaning out his
fingernails and everything. He got so particular that he
made the boss get somebody to iron his drawers. 'Cause,
boss, he said, I'm gonna beat that joker so he gonna look like
a can of beef tripe when I get finish with his no 'count butt.
. . . You sho' must be from down home, the way you talk
about trace chains, man, a brother said; he had his fingers
draped over the breasts of the young, cute girl sitting next to
him. Whar' you from, man, the brother said. Let the man
finish, someone said. . . . So when that Monday finally
came, the poet continued, he took a big swig from the beer
mug. When that Monday rolled around, everybody from all
over the state, this was in Georgia, came to see the Big
Fight. That bad nigger Kocomo was already there. He had
ripped up some trees by their roots and throw'd them about
a couple miles to the side, and was at the time throwing a
fifty-pound sledge hammer a mile or so up in the air and
every time the hammer came down, it buried itself around
five feet in the ground. And big Kocomo would reach down,
snatch it up, and send dirt flying everywhichaway.

Thousands of people were standing around watching this
and waiting for Efan. Efan was late. Then here come Efan
and his master and Miss Ann in a fine golden coach driven
by six fine black horses—not white ones, but *black* horses!
When Efan saw that bad nigger Kocomo, he start tremblin'
all over again. Great God! he thought to himself, if I don't
think up somethin', that bad nigger gonna kick my ass and
bury *me* in the ground like he doing that sledge hammer. He

didn't know what to do, he was trembling so. The crowd was
yelling. Efan looked at the bad nigger, and then spat in the
dust. Then he climbed out of the coach, and as he stepped
out, he flung off his cape. The crowd grew silent. Kocomo
was about five times bigger than Efan, but the way Efan was
carrying himself had everybody thinking he was bad too.
The crowd watched Efan in silence and anticipation, watched
Efan stroll calmly over to where this ex-gorilla was standing
with the sledge hammer. Efan walked over to the sledge
hammer that was lying at Kocomo's feet. He tried to lift it,
but it wouldn't budge. But he didn't try too hard because he
didn't want everybody to know exactly how weak he was.
When he saw that he couldn't possibly lift the thing, he
looked up to heaven, and with one hand on the handle of the
hammer, he said: St. Peter, you hear me talking to you up
there? Well, move over, and tell Sister Mary and them other
sisters to move out of the way, okay? And move Baby Jesus
too. When Kocomo heard this he start thinking, this sho' must
be a bad nigger, to be talking like that. And so he got scared
and start trembling a little bit himself. Then Efan reached
down like he was gonna pick up the hammer again, but
stopped and looked down at his hands. Then he looked over
to the coach to where the master and Miss Ann sat, and he
started walking over toward them. Everybody's eyes were
glued on him as he took his time going over to the coach.
Kocomo start to trembling, 'cause he didn't know what that
nigger was gonna do next. He was fixin' to run, because he
was sorta convinced already that there was something odd
about this little-bitty nigger who think he can beat somebody five times his size. Efan finally got to the coach,
climbed inside, and took Miss Ann's hand, and led her out so
that they were both in full view of the crowd. Then he

slapped her across the face. You could hear the slap crack like bullwhip. Efan said, Woman, didn't I tell you not to let me forget my white leather gloves. Where is my gloves at, huh? Now when Kocomo saw this, he jump up and start running. Lord have mercy, he said, any nigger slap a white woman in Georgia is too bad for me. And they never seen that bad Kocomo since.

"Okay," Doc said, getting up. They walked out into the cool night air. George noticed a clock peering out the back window of a silent store; it was 2:30.

seven

At the portal to Café Royale, Doc said good night to George. George expected as much; Doc, he knew, was an early riser. George was not an early riser. He would spend the rest of the night in Café Royale; if he met some woman he liked, he would go home with her; if he didn't, he would leave the café, which closed, at 5:30 a.m. and go around to the Coffee Shop and have breakfast with the cooks; and he would walk home early when the city would not yet be fully awakened, and the air fresh and the mist wet on his face, and he would sleep until one or two and then he would rise and go to the Drop Inn for something to eat.

As he walked into the main room, which was at the end of thirty descending steps, down in the belly of the sleeping city, his ears caught the familiar offbeat music from the off-key piano, which was being pounded on, as usual, by an old man left over from the Roaring Twenties. Except when some drunk usurped, the old man played undanceable pieces that ended only when he was exhausted, pieces George felt he should be doing the Charleston to but the congested dance floor wouldn't allow it. The room was jammed with buttocks, sometimes soft, sometimes hard, elbows jutting here and there, sharp-cornered tables that poked you in the ribs if in dancing you tried to gyrate your rear too obscenely. Waitresses darted daringly in and out the square holes left by the elbows. In the right far corner, a hand slipped under some lady's dress and didn't come back out. George felt an arm around his neck and turned only to become more encircled into it. A girl's lips were an inch from his.

"Hello," he said to the red lips.

The girl's lips remained only slightly open. George thought she was dancing with him—maybe she was. She rested her head on his neck and let out a little sigh. He felt her hand unzipping his zipper, and the hand was like a sock as it finally tightened up around his cock. He asked the girl if she wanted him to take her home. She shook her head slowly, sleepily. Are you drunk? Do you wanna dance? The pretty, yellow head shook twice.

"What do you want."

"I got what I want," she said, and gave his penis a tighter yet softer squeeze.

"Yes, but I want it too," he said, jerking himself out of her grasp. He saw three girls sitting at a table throw their heads and arms up in laughter. When the girl left him, she joined them at the table. She said something to them and they laughed again. He went to the bar to get a beer, feeling as though he had just wrestled with an animal. He leaned back on the bar. At one table were five Greenland Danes; they looked like Chinamen or Eskimos, and they didn't speak to the Danes, although they surreptitiously eyed the fat asses of the Danish girls as they passed. George felt a sudden warmth toward this group of what was certain, un-willful misfits; they were Danish, yet they were discriminated against by the Danes. They had now begun to sing in a loud voice, and a few people turned to look. One of them, with a mug in one hand, mounted the table, which was steadied by the others, and began screaming the song, which, presumably, was particular to Greenland, at the top of his voice; it was as though he were screaming to be noticed by the other Danes, screaming to be accepted—screaming at wooden planks, nevertheless. By the Danish standards of looks, these Greenlanders were certainly, to say the least, strange-looking. So why did they come to Denmark at all? Because they are Danish, too. (He began to think about Miss Smith at the American embassy. The money, why had she given him the money? He couldn't believe she was operating on guilt feelings, it had to be something much more shoddy than that.)

He stood at the bar, sucking the beer in through his teeth, digging on an attractive girl in white. She had very black hair that was tied at the nape of her neck, and she was newly suntanned. Her face, although thin, was very sensual. She looked very young. The girl was chatting with friends. He would make his way over through the crowd and ask her for a dance.

When she turned her face on him, he was astonished at how nervous he had gotten. She was intelligent, young, virginal, she had come to this place by mistake. She had, he noticed for the first time as she stood, the largest breast without being too large that he'd seen in a long time. As he danced with her, he was very excited. For a minute or two, he was completely unable to think of what he could possibly say to her that would not make him sound like a cock hound; the girl was nice, he had to be nice to her; she was young. He began to ask her questions softly into her ear, and she began to give him answers softly in his. She was an art student, she was from the country, she'd just returned from France with her father; she'd quit the Danish Academy of Art, because they "preach too much"—(see, independent, intelligent, nice, nice); she had just come to Copenhagen yesterday to live in an apartment her father and brother had found for her; they also built her an easel, a bed, and painted the room; her father was a farmer, who wanted his daughter to be a good painter.

"Well, what about you," she said, throwing her head back, looking him brightly in his eyes, although his own eyes were weary from too much beer and not enough sleep. He said he was a student, he tried to make it sound all right.

"Where do you live," she asked, as though she expected him to say in the train station, or the street.

"In the train station," he said, lying so naturally that it surprised him.

"You don't have a place to stay," she exclaimed. Oh no, he did have a place to stay: he checked his bag in at the train station, and he slept on the bench.

"That's no place to sleep," she protested. But he had run out of money, he had gone to the American embassy and had been told very harshly that he would be sent home if matters came to that, and they would have come to that if he didn't get out of the city very soon; furthermore, he had been unsuccessful at daily attempts to get a job—any kind of job.

"You can stay with me until you find a place," she said. Naturally he was overwhelmed.

"You have to promise me one thing: that you won't be naughty. I only have one room, and only one bed, you see?"

"I'll sleep on your sofa," he offered.

"I don't have a sofa."

"I don't mind the floor. I'll put a blanket on the floor and it'll be just as good."

"But you have to promise."

"I promise," he said.

"What's your name?"

"Efan," he said.

"Mine's Michele," she said as they left the small space they had occupied on the dance floor.

"This is Efan," she said to her friends, "he doesn't have a place to stay."

"I have a place for you," one of the young men said.

"He is going to stay with me," Michele said. "Besides, I have a secret for him." They all laughed, except Efan, who was still getting over his initial lie. He told lies so fast that he used to wonder if he could ever tell the truth—that is, he would really have to *think* about it before he could really tell someone what his *real* name was.

"Oh no, not that," Michele said, laughing, "I mean a *real* secret. You'll see," she said in George's direction.

As they walked along the streets toward her house, Michele leaned on his shoulder and began to tell him the story of the man who owns the house, which was a kind of Spanish castle, she shared with nine other girls. He was a hero, shot down some planes, killed some Germans; he was a nihilist, cared for nothing, or anybody; and he had seduced all the girls in the house, all except her, of course. When one became his mistress, she said, he reduced her rent. (As she babbled on about how interesting Mr. Niefson was, George began to sense jealousy sneaking up behind him. The idea of living in a house with nine women running around, strange women too, appealed to him very much, and he didn't want to share that pleasure with any man.)

Michele's room with the early-morning light glowing at the window was blue and quiet. No, don't turn the lights on, George said. If they turned on the light or even made any more noise than they were making, they'd wake up the room, disturb the sleeping bed, shock the blue stillness, that lay over it like sleep, into awareness.

"Are you a poet," Michele said.

"Well, yes," he said.

"We can have tea," Michele said, but George protested.

"Let's go to sleep," he said. "Do you have a blanket for me?" He felt suddenly sleepy, and wanted to lie in the house quietly, so quietly that one might hear the other eight girls breathing in their sleep. What were they like, anyway?

"Don't sleep on the floor," Michele whispered.

"Where am I to sleep then?"

"Here with me," she said, patting the small cot lightly, "but you must promise not to be naughty. You promise?"

Yes. Of course he did. He couldn't keep from laughing, from laughing at how well the girl played the game. She brought out some covers and converted the sofa into a sleepable bed; she pulled back the covers.

"I am going to take off my clothes and put on my nightgown, okay," she said, warning him in the nervous voice of the young virgin.

"Sure," he said, "I won't look."

"Oh, don't be silly."

"Well, I'm not looking. Do you want me to look, or what?" With his arms folded over his head, he peeped through a triangular crack and saw the girl stepping out of her pants; for a few seconds he lay watching her long thin legs that made parallel strips across his triangular keyhole.

"You're peeping, aren't you," she said.

"No. I'm not interested in making love to you. I just want to sleep," he said.

"Do you think we can sleep together without making love," she said, now standing with the light mute and blue at her side.

"Of course," he said, trying to make her sound ridiculous.

"All right, we are going to just sleep, is that right," she asked; a black shadow fell across her face and you couldn't know if she was smiling when she said this or what; maybe she really meant it. She lay on the bed beside him and pulled the covers up over them. He had noticed that she was wearing a very short, diaphanous thing, which she probably wore only on special occasions, for she had had to go to a top drawer for it; but he couldn't detect if she was completely nude underneath it.

"Good night, Efan," she said.

"Good night, Michele," said he.

He pretended he was asleep; then he began to count the seconds; when she was asleep or five minutes was up—whichever came first, he would casually lay his hand on her thigh, and then from the thigh to her stomach, from there to her breast, from there . . . He opened his eyes, and looked at her face hidden in the shadow; her large, sensual lips lay only inches from his; he kissed her and she didn't stir. Then he did it: he lay his hand on her thigh. It lay there a full three seconds, and at the end of those seconds he breathed easily, sighed: Wow, he'd made it. It was like having made an eight-foot leap across the mouth of a two-mile deep gorge. At the end of the fifth second, however, the hip stirred.

"I thought you were asleep," she said.

"I thought *you* were asleep," he said, reproaching her and at the same time attempting to excuse his breach of the treaty. They both fell silent again. Five seconds passed, ten seconds, and he began his tricks again. From the thigh to the stomach, etc. He felt certain this time, however, that she was awake and playing the game to the hilt, probably laughing this very minute, as his hand crept up her thigh. What was needed was something to break the convention, to shatter the glass house they had constructed. He thought of something.

"Hey, you awake?" he asked politely.

"No," she said.

"What about that secret?"

"Oh, yes, I was just thinking about it."

"What is it?"

"It's all wrapped up in my identity," she said. Good: they were finally talking about something; the silence of pretending to be asleep was something too oppressive. In fact, already his hand had made the infamous leap and was now imperceptibly caressing her ass.

"You mean I won't know the secret until I get to know you?" he asked.

"No, it doesn't directly have to do with my past. Oh, yes it does. It's difficult to say."

"Well, then, just tell me what it is," he said as his hand crossed a line of elastic, which definitely answered the question of her nudity.

"I don't know if I should. I mean at first I thought you would be surprised, then I thought you would be mad (I don't know that you'd be mad). Look, I'll give you hints. You can guess," she compromised.

"Did you sleep with your old man?"

"No."

"The last time a girl went through this secret bit with me, she had made it with her old man. It broke me up. I don't know why," George said; he was ruminating while at the same time he was stroking the girl's breast, and his penis was stiffening.

No, it was not that, she said, nor had she made it with her brother, nor with her forty-five-year-old uncle, and she wasn't pregnant—all this came to his ear like a song. So what is it?

"I'll give you a hint."

"What is the hint," he asked as he felt the breast awakening in his hand; she had now placed her head on his folded arm, and her legs had parted. He sensed something weird, something mysterious, unconscionable, unpermissible, unspeakable—so he concentrated on his hands, her body, the warmth of her smooth inner thighs. She began to breathe heavily, and he knew that the secret, which, if it were terrible enough, revealing enough, though it would normally embarrass or shock him or make him repulse the girl (which was all she was afraid of), would now spur him on, would make him disrespect her, yes, but on a deeper level, where hate and disrespect and violence were dynamite for blasting one's way into the unconscious where orgasms live.

"One hint is . . ." He carefully caressed her hot stomach. Beginning to pant somewhat more audibly than before, she suddenly slung her opened mouth before his, her lips full, hot, liquid.

"What is the hint," he asked, controlling his quivering voice, as he slid his hand from where the hair began to grow around her pussy across the juicy, hot, almost-grasping cunt to her asshole, where he lodged his index finger.

"Ouch!"

Damnit, he forgot to cut his fingernails!

"It is about your family and my family," she said, getting

out the full sentence before collapsing into moans and gut-
tural sounds.

What! were they brothers and sisters, would he fuck his
sister! Yes, he would fuck his sister if he had a sister which
he didn't have. I am fucking my sister, he said to himself,
happily.

"You are not my sister, right?"

"Oh no, nnnooooo, oh, God, that's goood."

"Give me another hint," he said, slipping down her panties.

"It has to do with You and Africa and Me. A long time
ago," she said. "Oh, God, Oh, Oh, Oh."

"I know. You love to get fucked by Africans, you went to a
dance and got fucked by three different Africans in the
course of the evening behind the dark building, right." His
cock was hard as a stone now, hard as a nail. The rough
head of it went up into the soft juicy part of her cunt. He
could not care less about her secret, he was about to pounce
on her and fuck his ass off, when she bellowed out.

"Oh, God, do you want me to tell you!!"

"What is it!!!" He flew up suddenly on his knees, his cock
in his hard-gripped hand.

"Do you really want to know!" she heaved spasmodically.
She was teasing in the way she said it.

"Yes," he shouted back, half unconscious of what he was
saying or what they were even talking about, as he threw
her legs open and thrust himself forward into her.

"AAAAIIIEEEE. I'm gonna tell ya, I'm gonna tell ya."

"Okay, okay do it, do it now." His cock was halfway in
her and she was screaming like mad. He was afraid she
would come too soon; he was afraid *he* might come too soon.

"Oh yes, oh yes. Here it is, here it is," she bellowed; she

was procrastinating, temporizing, she was obviously trying to synchronize the revelation with her orgasm, and George knew she was not more than a good ten seconds from coming. And the secret would come. What would it be?

"Oh, oh, I tell you now, I—I—" She was trying, but the come was beginning to break loose into her body, beginning to make her tremble with epileptic vibration all over, she began to fuck with her ass and take up again the task of synchronizing.

"Oh, I—I—am—" She was definitely coming now, and he shot himself up into her with such force that he lost his grip on the wooden gate that held the snorting, thundering bull in his stall until the matador and his muleta was ready, that hand slipped, and he felt the razor-sharp back of the bull as it passed under his hand.

"What's the Secret, Bitch!!!" he screamed.

"AAAAIIIIEEEE OOOOOHHHHH I—I—AM AM AA-AAIIIIEEEE."

"GODDAMN YOU, WHAT IS IT, BITCH."

"AAAAIIIIEEE I I—AM A NIGGER, I AM A NEGRO," she screamed, and began to come like crazy.

"Oh God," he said, coming, "you nigger bitch, you nigger bitch come, nigger." She seemed already to have been coming a full four minutes, and when he called her nigger she came again.

Later, when the room was much lighter, she explained to him how three of her generations ago her great-grandmother had had a baby by a black man from Africa, a man who was a sailor and who had come to their little port city, like some American G.I. who ends up in the Cassanova; as a consequence, some of the members of her family—her brother, for example, had very coarse hair and dark skin; she herself

only had the coarse hair; George studied a picture of the
brother, it was amazing that he looked like an American Negro. Most of the offspring, however, could pass for undiluted
Danes, as the girl certainly had before his own discern-
ing eyes. Now, with light in the room, he looked at her carefully. She had the large lips, yes, the slightly coarse hair now
that he looked at it carefully, she had a little of the nose, she
looked like an Italian, and he couldn't tell about the skin
because she had a recent suntan, but he didn't think she had
the skin color. He lay on his back, looking at the light creep-
ing in the room, he didn't know what he thought about it, it
certainly made him horny, he wanted to fuck the girl again,
call her nigger and feel her come with a frequency and
pleasure she'd never had before, and feel himself come that
way too, like fucking one's mother or sister. It was certainly
incestuous. But it would wear off, he was afraid it would
wear off. It would probably be gone by the afternoon, or
right after they had eaten breakfast, probably be gone by
the time they fucked again and the fuck would be normal.
They fucked again, fast, quick like animals, she screamed
nigger, and he said it softly into her ear, they both came
several times, several impulsive, satisfying times.

He fell asleep afterwards, and had a dream about Miss
Smith. It all took place in the year 1593. Miss Smith was
Queen Elizabeth, Ned Green was Sir Walter Raleigh, he himself was Spenser, at other times Sir Walter, whose amorous
attacks on the queen were impending; there was Doc, who
played the part of some serious comic satirist like John
Marston or Jonson. There was one scene which was very
vivid. He (this was when he was Walter Raleigh) and the
queen were walking in the gilt-laden corridor when he suddenly reached down and ran his hand under Elizabeth's

long, floor-sweeping gown; he grabbed her in the cunt and discovered she was wearing no panties and that she was wet as hell. He remembered thinking in the dream, Here is your big chance to promote your new book (*The Faerie Queene*) —he was, of course, now seeing himself as Spenser. He put his fingers to his nose. He remembered that it smelled just like ordinary pussy. He remembered also that the queen hit him on the nose with her fan (something Othello had given her, one heard of that sort of thing in court) and confided to him that she had a secret. When asked what the secret was, she replied that it was that his head was to be cut off. He had only two alternatives: he could kill the queen and maybe foist the thing on someone else, Marlowe or some idiot like Marston, or he could forceably fuck the queen, and fuck her so well that she would pardon him, would spare his head because he had a golden dick (that was the phrase that came to him in his dream—or was it afterwards). The latter alternative, he decided, was more likely to assure him of his head remaining on his shoulders; so he chose it. He tripped the queen with his foot, and when she fell to the cushioned floor, he was between her legs; he had to work fast, he had to be in her before (1) she screamed and/or (2) someone came. It was a great relief of anxiety to him when he finally felt his length in her, and felt her definitely coming. He watched the eyes of the queen—the eyelids fluttering, the blue eyes soft under them fluttering as she screamed the fanfare of her coming through the slumbering ears of the court. When he looked down at his penis, he saw that it had turned gold. He had a Golden Cock. He remembered thinking with magnanimity that he had the only Golden Cock in the kingdom. It felt like a slug of lead, but it was the gold of the sun.

That was the Queen/Miss Smith's secret—that he could have had a Golden Cock if he were willing to risk—"willing to work with your hands"—to risk his neck. Yeah, that's why Miss Smith was acting so strange!

When he woke up, sunlight flooded his face. He turned over and discovered that there was a girl, another girl standing before him, offering him what looked like a soft-boiled egg in an egg cup. As it turned out, that was precisely what it was: breakfast. Served by one of Michele's friends (she was with Michele last night when she and George met), who agreed to make him breakfast while Michele went shopping. George was very pleased that she could clear up his confusion with such direct explanations. As he lay in bed propped on an elbow eating his egg, the girl, who said she was Viebeka, leaned back in a chair. She had allowed her dress to slide back down her thighs, and it was all George could do to prevent himself from staring into her crotch. Tired of fighting himself, George began to study the girl's crotch. She had on red panties, and he was close enough to notice they had a knitted pattern. As he stared at the panties, he answered a few questions about where he came from and where he was going. With her legs open, the girl answered a few of his questions too.

When she finally got up to take the plate back into the kitchen, he threw himself back on the cot with relief; his eyes had become sore from staring and he had to massage some light into them. She returned and got in the same identical position. It was as though he had been fucking her in a position which they both thought was very good and she had said, Wait a minute, and got up and went to the john to piss and came back and got in the same position again. He felt the girl was trying to get him to fuck her. This time when he looked up her open legs, he saw that when she had gone into the kitchen to take back the plate she had also taken off her panties. He got up, dressed quickly. Said good-bye and that he'd call Michele later.

eight

When George walked into the living room of the house where he rented a small room, his landlady was in hysterics.

"You better call lady," she was saying, trying to make her near-unclear English clearer by doing a brief pantomime act of someone on the telephone. She was about sixty, with fire-red hair that stood out from her head like wire springs. He had never seen her without a cigar.

"Lady call." Who might that "lady" be? His landlady finally brought a slip of paper. It was a telephone number.

"Okay, thank you, Mrs. Andersen," he said. He gave her a 25-kroner piece, picked up the telephone, and dialed the number. Surprised to discover that he had called the American embassy, he waited somewhat apprehensively as the receptionist connected him to the consul.

"Oh, hello," he said when the consul's voice came through.

"Now," she began, "where have you been, Mr. Winthrop, you were supposed to come by my office this morning, I had a job for you, don't you want to work; I am absolutely furious with you, and to be frank, a little bit disappointed. Now, can you explain to me where you have been?"

"I am sorry, Miss Smith, I was under the impression that—"

"Where have you been, Mr. Winthrop, you know I didn't *give* that money to you; you owe that money to the embassy, and you are obliged to, at the least, to be courteous and to show some interest in getting a job to pay it back."

"Miss Smith," George said, angry, "I don't owe you any-

thing. You *gave* that money to me, as far as I am concerned."

"Mr. Winthrop, I have gone too far out on the limb for
you already. I am under no obligation to do for you what I
have done. I arranged this morning for you to help the de-
livery men with the unloading, but when I looked for you,
called you several times, you were not to be found; so, then I
gave up on that, and arranged for you to be one of the bar-
tenders for tonight, but it's two o'clock before I can get in
contact with you, and now someone else has the job."

"I wasn't looking for that kind of work," George said.

"Are you above that kind of work, Mr. Winthrop, just because you went to college?"

"You're fucking right," he said, slamming the phone down.
Apologize! Shit. Apologize for what?

"You pay money now," Mrs. Andersen was saying, standing only inches away, puffing away in clots of blackness on a
cigar like an old antiquated steaming locomotive as it stood
immobile on a steel platform at the country fair.

"Yeh, I pay a little now," George said, half to himself; he
had told the landlady that previous morning he was going to
borrow some money from a friend, and she undoubtedly
thought Miss Smith was that friend; and besides he had to
give her something to show his good faith. He gave her 50
of the 250 crowns he owed her, and to his surprise she was
immensely pleased. She bowed *"tak"* and offered him a cigar, shaking her red head comically and speaking in an
ecstatic flow of Danish. He realized later that her great
gratitude was due to her previous fear that he, being black,
might not have paid her anything at all—for most Scandi-
navians, being great and hopeless importers of American

theories, did not trust black people. (So what, he didn't trust the Scands either.)

He found himself walking down some street, some pleasant street, where flowers were being sold; his eye began to study the forms of the people. A woman bending to examine a basket of tomatoes. Two Danish nymphs. He came to a bridge. Some people were out rowing on a nice day. The sky beautiful blue and clean and unmarred by machines. The fresh smell of rain come and gone early in the morning like Santa Claus whom you missed but knew was definitely there by the exciting smell of the things left. He was asleep and someone (his brother Corn—the mudderfucker) threw a bucket of ice-cold water in his face. That was the freshness of the breeze, the after-rain smell walking on that bridge. He stopped and looked at himself shaking on the flimsy surface of the water. Shaking because someone in a boat was too near. He was not afraid, though. Mainly because nobody can get too close (wish to God they could). Except words maybe, but he could work with words. Words, however, had misunderstood him. Many times, too many times. So it was best that he only act, and leave the interpretation to his actions. Cut words out—for, after all, who needs the interpretations of words.

This Jewish boy, with the brown, near-red beard, whom he was always glad to meet in some street. This scared Jewish boy, who was writing a letter (it was now fifty pages long) to his semi-illiterate (his phrase) parents in Los Angeles who own thirty apartment houses in Watts and whom he feared his letter (his exile, his alienation, his legacy if he had to have one) would be wasted upon. Good choice of word, wasted. This Jewish boy, his own age. This Jewish boy, who said (asked), you would not fuck (I mean not even if she asked you or if you knew you could if you wanted to) my girl would you; asked it because he knew how badly Danish women wanted to fuck whatever black man they could, like any young man at times wanted to fuck whatever woman he could. Asked it, begged it. And got the wrong answer.

"Hey, how many have you fucked so far?"

"Oh, cut it out. Don't bullshit."

No, the Jewish boy is serious. It's terrible to be this way, isn't it (George thinks). He is afraid, the Jewish boy is too near. This Jewish boy is trying to cheapen his action, trying to reduce it to a figure, trying to use it for something else, something which it is not. The sociologist, trying to infer. Kick his motherfucking ass!!! And anybody else who pulls that bullshit on me! How did you get to Princeton! How did *you* get there yourself, Mother Fucker (careful articulation, you did?), walk?

"Look, man," George said, "I'll see you later."

"You gonna be here this winter. I'm counting on you for intellectual companionship," the Jewish boy said.

"I'm trying to get outa this town, man."

"You not going back to the States, are you?"

"I think so."

"Oh, this is terrible."

"Yeh, but I wanna do it."

"Well, if you don't, I'll see you around."

"Yeah."

So he went back up the street, the strangely beautiful street. And he found himself (happily) at his door. Driven back. By something in the ugly-ass Jewish cat. When he got to the top of the stairs, he almost stumbled over something. He looked down, and discovered his suitcase with its mouth

half open, and his clothes stuffed in it. He stood there. So I
have been kicked out. Now, what I should do is pick up my
shit and run, and I won't have to pay the rest of the rent, he
thought. But when he had given her the money only a few
hours ago, she seemed very pleased. Why had she done this?
She had no right to throw his things out like that! He put his
key in the door and opened it.

nine

He was standing in the doorway with the key in his hand, and he faced the landlady and two policemen.

Whiipp!! Just like that, like a bird's beak darting for a bread crumb, the old lady had his key out of his hand. She stood there with her legs apart, her clenched fists on her bony, unperceptible hips, and puffed out three clots of stinking smoke, which he later decided was a signal (a kind of Morse code), for at that very moment the police grabbed him. He kept thinking that the landlady was a Chicago gangster who had made good and had come over to Copenhagen and set up business under the disguise of a woman. That would explain the red wig and the cigar.

The policemen took him outside the door. One of them, having stuffed his clothes into the suitcase, put his foot on it and locked it. They went down the stairs. George was thinking that if his clothes weren't properly packed his suitcase was surely going to burst, because it wasn't a very good one. He wanted to tell the policemen that very much, but he felt a strange sense of speechlessness. One of the policemen opened the back door of the car and he got in, and the suitcase came in behind him. He immediately opened it and began to poke the many tongues of clothes back in. He looked up and noticed that the car was not moving. The policemen were talking in Danish; one of them said something about the landlady's cigar and pinched his nose. George started to tell them his theory about her being a Chicago gangster, but he felt speaking in English (he would have botched it in Danish) might have made them think he had been eavesdropping; and he wanted to be as nice to them as he could. Suddenly the policemen put their elbows across the seat and turned to him.

"Let me see your passport," the driver said, with an English accent.

George gave it to him.

While the one examined his passport, George said to the other one, trying for friendliness, "She called you, huh?"

"Ah, that old bag," the policeman said; he was the one who had pinched his nose; the way he said "that old bag" made it clear that his English was not as good as the driver's; this policeman was much younger, and George suspected he was not as educated or widely traveled as the other, and yet he seemed much nicer.

"When I gave her fifty crowns this morning, not even two hours ago, she seemed pleased. I told her I was gonna pay her all of it tomorrow, and I thought she believed me. I don't understand it," George said to the younger policeman.

"Ya, she's an old bag," the policeman replied, friendly, obsequious.

"You know, you may have to leave Copenhagen," the other policeman said.

"Why? I haven't done anything."

"You haven't any money either. So, you cause trouble for Danish citizens. For other people, too."

"She's no citizen, that bitch is a gangster."

"Still, you don't have a job?"

"Of course, I have a job."

"You do, what?"

"I work at the American embassy. I—I—just got a job working as a bartender. I got it yesterday, and I am supposed to go to work tonight."

"Really," the older policeman said, "that's very strange. It's bloody strange indeed. Still, we will have to keep your passport, so that you cannot leave the city legally; you will have to contact us when you have a new address—"

"Don't go back there," the younger policeman said, smiling. George felt he was trying in his own way to mitigate whatever harshness the other had implied, still trying to maintain that brochure reputation of Danish hospitality. "She's a real old bag, *ni, ni,*" he said.

"How can I get a place without a passport?"

"We can put you up for the night," the older one said, grinning in the way American policemen grin when they think they have said something witty, which by definition is vicious.

"It don't make no difference. Just tell 'em call our station. I'll give you the number, it'll be all right," the young one said apologetically. He gave George a slip of paper.

"We'll let you know in a couple days if you have to leave or not," the driver said. George got out of the car.

"Farvel," the young Dane said as the car pulled away.

Farvel hunky motherfuckers.

George and his bulging suitcase made it to a telephone booth. He called Miss Smith at the American embassy.

"I am sorry about what happened this morning," he said. She said nothing back. He waited long enough.

"I was picked up by the police a few minutes ago," he said. Still, she said nothing back. A strange bitch. Heartless. It was as though by her silence she was saying, Yes, this is what one can expect of niggers.

"Are you there?" he asked.

"Yes."

"I was saying I got picked up by the police, and they

wanted to kick me out because I don't have any money, so I told them I had a job at the embassy as a bartender; you think I could still get the job?"

"I'll see what I can do, but you'd better come right over here immediately. You'd better *run*."

"I got kicked out of my place, too; what do you think I should do with my suitcase?"

"Bring it along, I'll have to get you a place to live too, I guess."

George caught a tram right where he was. As he sat looking out the window, he remembered the girl (what's her name) . . . Michele, and decided that he could probably stay with her, if the shit really hit the fan. *You'd better run!* That bitch must be jumping up and down right now, thinking that she had the nigger running like a puppet on a string; but if he ever got the chance he was gonna put the shit on her, but good! He needed her right now, because she could convince the police that he had a job. She could save him, like no one could, but when he was finished with her he was gonna fix her ass like it was never fixed before.

He began to think about the scared Jewish boy, who thought he was the Wandering Jew; he thought about Michele, whose father, although a farmer himself, wanted her to be a famous painter; and Doc, who as a doctor saw death every day and yet was more frightened of it than he; he thought of the Drop Inn, of Cassanova, of Café Royale, and all the lives that pass through them; he thought about his family on the farm in North Carolina, he thought about Old Red, who must be about twelve years old now and who had not pulled a plow in three years because of the tractors; it was a good life for Old Red, all he had to do was walk around and eat grass, eat hay in the winter. Except there was nothing to fuck. He had once seen Old Red trying to make it with a cow. Maybe he didn't need to fuck, now that he was retired. When you get old, you don't need it any more. It was probably a kind of relief, a relief from having to drill everything you see for about the first fifty years of your life. But he was young, and he wanted to know; he wanted to know as much as one could know; he already knew that one could never know an Answer. Even Death wasn't an answer to anything. The way one got around death, by the way, was to enjoy, enjoy every minute, and pray that when death came, it came quickly. Then, for no reason at all, he began to think about a girl he had met in Copenhagen a month ago; she was from Arizona, she was a missionary from some Presbyterian church; they were at a dance; he finger-fucked her outside the dance, in a shadow, she came, and he remembered thinking how nice she was, and that she was a missionary on her way to Africa; she cried when she left him, she said she liked him so much; and now, for the first time, he allowed himself to feel what he would not allow himself to feel that day standing at the bus stop as her bus pulled away. She was a simple and lovely person.

Still, he could not afford (could not allow) himself to be taken in by shit like that. The beloved was nobody's God but the weakling's, the suppliant. The God of the strong was the Lover, the Seducer. The only living force in the world was that of the Seducer. His grandmother might have said this, not his philosophy professor. The only way to keep your strength is to give; never accept anything from anybody. The 100 kroner was not something given to him; he had taken it, because he had (in his own way) seduced the consul; she had not given the money to him; she had surrendered it. She was going to surrender more. The Bitch.

When he walked into the consul's office, she was leaning back in her chair; there was the glint of victory in her eyes, she seemed younger, she wore the clothes of a coquette—a white silk blouse with a nice dip into her surprisingly full breast, a necklace that accentuated the dip by falling lazily into the valley between the mounts, and a lipstick that left her mouth glistering with juice, and a bit more full than usual. George felt offended by the woman's cosmetic effects. He settled into a chair near the door. The woman got up, closed the door, and sat on the corner of the desk. Her skirt was raised by what was meant to be an unconscious gesture. Her hand went through the formality of preparing a cigarette for smoking. Cigarette lit, the lady's hand went over to the desk, picked up an envelope, and delivered it to George. Folding the envelope in his hand, he continued to stare uninterrupted at the woman, who was very much a lady, stare at her like she was a witch, although he was taken in by the act of her store-bought beauty.

"Open it," she said, spraying smoke from her nostrils, like a female dragon. What annoyed him—(for that precisely was what it was, *annoyance*)—was the fact that she had pulled her dress up on him; she was showing him her thighs and there was nothing he could do about it; the skirt was only a few inches up her thigh, but it was as if she had thrown off all her clothes and was sitting there pretending nothing was wrong; it was an unfair thing to do; it was a definite attack on him, his masculinity and everything; he wanted to push the woman back on the desk, strip her of her panties, and give it to her right there on the desk. But: Cool it, Jiveass, cool it!

He opened the envelope and took out an American passport. He opened it and discovered it was his own.

The lady raised herself from the desk, strutted to the swivel chair, and threw herself in it.

"For the time being I have arranged for you to stay at the Hilton. Although this is somewhat a compensation for the discomfort I might have caused you, you will have to pay me back with whatever you earn here," she said.

This bitch doesn't really expect me to pay, does she?

He said nothing. He didn't think Miss Smith had any intention of making him pay, since the cost of living at the Hilton was exorbitant.

"You should cooperate with me," she said. "I could get you jobs, you owe me some—the embassy—a lot of money, you know."

"What do you want me to do, become a spy?"

"That's not a bad idea, except we would have to get the appointment from Washington." She laughed. Then she pushed a button on her desk.

A man poked his head in the door; Miss Smith said his name was Mr. Olsen. George shook his hand.

"Mr. Olsen will show you what you need to do at the bar," Miss Smith said.

He went out the door behind the cracker.

ten

It was the kind of party he imagined the head of the English department at a small private college in New England would throw. There were some attractive ladies, almost all of whom were married to some economical specialists or political analysts, or something. There were some handsome and un-handsome gentlemen, all attired in black suits and ties. They all squared into small groups like football huddles. There was plenty of liquor—too much. A waste. As the evening grew, the huddles got drunker and began to dwindle down into members of two's and three's. George had been coaxed, seduced into seven discussions of race problems, and had not come out too badly.

At one point, Miss Smith, who was looking ten years younger, which would make her thirty-two or so, came rushing up to the bar with a tail of men behind her.

"I can't stand old men," she whispered to George as he dropped a couple of ice cubes into her glass.

At another point, when he took a walk out on the terrace, George was accosted by a Mrs. Hamilton, who began to tell him how much she "admired" the Negro race. She was fairly drunk.

"You know you're very handsome, don't you," Mrs. Hamilton said. She was not a bad-looking piece. "My husband would kill me if he knew I said that to you, you know. It would be all right if I said it to any white man, because he doesn't really care; but if he knew I said it to you, a Negro, he'd kill me." The ice rattled nervously in her glass.

"Why?"

"Oh, don't be naïve, you know why!"

"Then why are you risking your life?"

"You are smart, I can tell that," she muttered. "Look, I have been so unfaithful to that man, and he knows it. I think he's keeping a toll, and when it gets to some mystic number that he has in his brain, chop, off with my head. How do I know, you may be that number?"

"What do you think I am—a stud?"

"Yes."

"Really, how do you know?"

"I can tell."

"I won't be your stud."

"You would if I gave you things."

"Oh, yeah?"

"Yeah."

"Oh, I don't want anything. I just think you're beautiful," George said.

"Here," she said, handing him her coaster. He took it, turned it over, and discovered a number written on the underside. He slipped it into his coat.

"Call me, any time you want, buddy boy," she said. Miss Smith came up.

"You can't have him, Mrs. Hamilton," she said jokingly. "He belongs to the embassy, he owes us so much money."

"Do you need a job, Paul," Mrs. Hamilton said.

"He has a job, which he is going to lose if he doesn't get in there and take care of it," Miss Smith said. "There are several people waiting in there for drinks. Including me." The three of them walked inside.

Ten minutes later Gloria walked in. "Oh, where have you been?" she exclaimed when she saw George.

"Here," he said.

"I've been asking Miss Smith about you, but she said she didn't know your address, but Dad said you might be here tonight. I left my date early to come over. It's really groovy meeting someone your own age around here; these people here can be a drag."

"When everybody here is drunk, let's go out on the town. I know some nice places. Listen, you smoke?"

"Yeah, can you get something?"

"I can get *anything*."

"God, I've been dying for some pot, ever since London."

"Yeh, they really smoke a lot in London."

"Yeah, don't they?"

"A lot of people, young people, smoke a lot here. You wouldn't think so, but they do."

"Oh, God, it's so exciting meeting someone like you, these people are such drags."

"Look, when I get a break I'll meet you out on the terrace," George said, handing her a gin and tonic.

He met Gloria on the terrace.

"Look, let's make it. Everybody in there is drunk. You got a car, right?"

"Yeah, let's make it."

They went to Nick's place and copped the stuff. George told her about the room that Miss Smith had reserved for him at the Hilton.

"Okay," she said. "If you can't get it for some reason, you let me rent one."

She stayed in the car while he went in. He came back in ten minutes with the key. They decided it would be best if she wasn't seen going in with him. When they were both finally in the room, they locked the door.

"Don't use the telephone," George told her. "They might be snooping, you know."

George surveyed the room, surveyed it in the way a general might cast a supercilious eye upon some newly conquered turf; the deep blood-colored carpet that ran like grass for about thirty feet from one side of the wall to the other shot him with a sense of victory; the slim Danish chairs, the table, the bed were his own quickly snatched treasure. Two nights ago, he was sleeping in a room about the size of a closet, in a terrible bed, and now he had a room with service; two nights ago, he was living the status of a pauper, now that of an American businessman. But American businessmen were nothing to imitate, for certain. Yet, he was impressed at the power of the imagination; the power of the active will to manifest itself into materials. The power of his own imagination.

He threw himself into one of the chairs and rolled some of the stuff. Taking a deep drag, he handed it to Gloria.

"You ever make love on pot?" she asked.

"Yeh, it was nice. You?"

"No," she said. "I would love to, though."

"Do you wanna order some food?"

"Wow, food!"

George picked up the phone and someone said that a menu could be found in the telephone desk.

"Let's order a lot of food, some of everything. I got a lot of money," Gloria said.

George ordered lobster, crab, roast duck, hors d'oeuvres, a bottle of French wine, raspberries with cream, and some American cigarettes.

George rolled, and they smoked. They giggled, time flew.

"Can I take off my dress," Gloria said. "It's making too much noise. I mean, you know what I mean."

George started laughing. He laughed for five minutes, though he thought it had lasted at least half an hour.

Gloria got up, unzipped her skirt, and let it fall to the floor; she had on black bikini panties and a red garter belt.

"Madam," George said, imagining himself as some count, "can I take off the garter belt?"

"Oh, with pleasure," the Lady replied. She came over to him, and he unfastened the belt, the whole process taking about fifteen minutes, according to Standard Pot Time.

The Gentleman looked up at the Lady, whose face was not chagrined, and said, "Can I try these," nodding toward her panties, which were only inches from his nose.

"Sure, in fact please," the Lady replied.

That took an hour, but it was worth it. By this time his cock was hard as the metal arm of the chair. The Gentleman found himself taking it out to show it to the Lady.

"Look," he said to the Lady.

"That's absolutely amazing," the Lady said. "Can I?"

Of course she could. The Lady bent down, and took it into her beautiful, wonderful, sweet, motherly, savage mouth. That took an hour.

"God," said the Lady upon rising and catching her breath shortly, "I never felt this way before."

"Allow me," the Gentleman said, as he fingered the tail of the Lady's blouse, and he began to slip the thing over the Lady's wonderful head, most beautiful head, and then he proceeded to unfasten the hooks of the bra that so well guarded her sacred, white, nay, alabaster breasts, those virgin does that fed . . . amongst the. . . . He worked as fast as he could, so that his attention would not waver; for he had decided that as soon as he had set the breasts free, he was going to pop the nipples into his mouth and crush them (ever so lightly) against the palate of his mouth as a connoisseur would a grape; it was something that he had made his mind up about, he had discussed it with no one; it was something he had to do, it was a duty, a responsibility; only if he were not distracted by a stray odor, the disorder of disheveled hair, or the syncopated breathing; it was something, he must . . .

"What's that . . ." the Lady said drunkenly, hornily; he had put his leg against her cunt and he could feel the heat and the wetness through the corduroy; the sweet cunt juices were coming on like hot lava.

He heard the knocking at the door too. They sat there looking puzzled at each other, thinking, What could that be? It seemed as though they sat there fifteen minutes.

It was only until a little voice said room service that they guessed that the food had arrived. George looked at the girl, Gloria, and saw that the girl was absolutely nude, naked; she was in no condition to have guests. So, he decided she should get behind the door, so that when he opened it to bring in the food, she would be hidden by the door. Sounded very clever, the whole thing. Taking her by the arm and placing a finger to his lip, he carried out the plan to a T.

Opening the door, he discovered a dining cart loaded with food and being presided over by a boy who had the face of an infant; he must be about two or three years old, George decided, give or take a couple months.

He said goodbye to the boy when he had the cart in the

room, but the boy wouldn't go away. George gave him five crowns from his pocket.

He looked at the food. It was a lot of food. The duck had her legs open. Out of nowhere, the girl, Gloria, came; she grabbed him around the neck, like she was trying to kill him by strangulation.

"Fuck me, oh, fuck me, I can't wait, oh, fuck me," the Lady said.

And as she dragged him to the bed, the Gentleman remembered his responsibility. He took the nipples (they had grown somewhat since he had last seen them, they were now teenagers) and took them between his teeth.

"Oh, oh, oh," the Lady said, tearing unladylike at his pants; whereupon the Gentleman, very gentlemanly, took them off. Now they were both very naked. He sucked on one of the Lady's nipples for an hour. He was a baby at her breasts. The Lady couldn't wait any longer; she grabbed his cock and stuck it in the juicy mouth of her pussy.

"Fuck me, please fuck me," she said. But for some reason the Gentleman held back; he was thinking about his responsibility, he had finished only half of his duty; there was the other nipple puffed out as hard as an apple and as yet unsucked. He grabbed it with his teeth, and as he did so the Lady (that impetuous Lady) reached up and grabbed his ass by both buns and in he went.

"Oh, God," he said, and forgot his responsibility forever. They fucked, they fucked.

"Wait," said the girl, for she was no longer a Lady. She then got up on her knees. They fucked, they fucked.

"Oh, Oh, OOOOOOHHHHHH," the girl said, coming.

"Wait," George said. Too late.

eleven

When he finally woke up the next day, Gloria was not there; there was a note for him on the food cart. He picked up the note, looking at the cart of food; one of the duck's legs was missing. The note read as follows:

> Tried to wake you up, couldn't, so—I have to get home, and give some excuse; what, I don't know. I left some money to take care of the food; here's my number Tr 2365. Call me around 3. That's the greatest I've ever had it; you were beautiful. How long did it last; call me—
>
> Gloria

He looked at the currency; it was two American twenties.

He lay on the bed resting for about an hour; he saw that it was about one. He got dressed and went downstairs in the lobby and bought a *New York Times*. He came back into the room and saw that the room had a radio and television. He turned the television on, and turned it off; then he turned the radio on, to some music that sounded like Vivaldi. He lay on the bed with the paper. The paper said it was George Washington's birthday, February 22. He looked at a picture of a parade somewhere in America. Then the radio was speaking in English; it said something about Malcolm X. George jumped up on the bed. He couldn't believe what the radio had said. He listened carefully. ". . . shot down by unknown assassins, in the Audubon Ballroom in Harlem, as he was about to address a group . . ." The announcer had a

German accent, he could have been speaking German which George couldn't understand, but the message was clear; George was sitting on the bed, his ears straining for help from the radio, and then he heard the clicking of a key in the door. He sat there looking at the door as it came open and Miss Smith came in. George sat there looking at the door, and it could have been anybody walking in the door. The woman closed the door and came over to the bed; she took off her coat.

"I want to talk to you," she said, putting on her phony maternal accent.

"Malcolm is dead," George said, still looking at the door.

"You left with Gloria last night, and her father hasn't seen her since; the whole embassy is upset. These people are not used to interracial—"

George reached and took the woman's chin in his hand; he thought he would choke her, but his mind did something else instead. He could see clearly that the woman was prepared to seduce him; that was why she came to his room; that was why the room was his; that was why she had her own key. He was thinking that maybe he should deprive her of that pleasure. His hands went down into her blouse which was more like a man's shirt and went around her very large breasts. There was something hard at the back of his head, as he sent his hand up her skirt. The woman's panties were wet.

"I am old enough to be your mother," she said, sounding like somebody's mother about to be made by someone who could be her son; and yet he knew she wanted it more than he; he knew that the woman was wishing this was incest, and he knew that what she had said only added fuel to her flames.

"Yes, I could be your son," he said, pulling her skirt down. He was sitting on the bed, and the woman was standing in front of him. He was feeling that she wanted to be undressed. "Yet you want it, don't you; you came here for it, didn't you?"

The woman flung her mouth into his. She thrust her tongue down his throat. She had the strength of a strong man; he knew that she must have bitten into his skin, because he tasted blood. With one hand she tore into his pants and grabbed his cock, with a grip so passionate that he screamed, only to have the sound drunk by her voracious mouth. Gloria was a girl and when she put her hand on his cock she only put her hand on it; but this woman was a woman; when she put her hand on his cock, he almost died with pleasure; he thought for a moment he was going to come right in her hand. She began to breathe like a bull, and then she stood up and slipped out of her panties; still in her white blouse, she leaped on his cock, grabbing it, jabbing herself with it, finally getting it in, and then pulling it up in her as far as it would go, she let out a scream that sounded like an attacking Indian. Then it was obvious to George that the woman was having a tremendous orgasm. She came for what seemed like a full two and a half minutes. She moaned long and lowly like a wolf; whereas Gloria measured her comes in Oh, Oh, Oh's, Miss Smith came in deeply satiating Ah's. George had never been with a woman who came so quickly and yet so slowly. He had the impression that this woman was one who didn't fuck often but when she did she enjoyed it as few women did; it was not a social ritual with this red-neck from Oklahoma; it was a need; the thought of this gave George pleasure; the earnestness and sincerity and self-indulgence with which the woman had come flattered

him. He felt a deep joy in thinking that he would like to fuck
her forever.

Still there was the numbness at the back of his head, just
beneath the head, where the neck starts. It was as though he
had been lobotomized.

He flipped the woman over on her back, and began taking
off his own clothes; when he finished, he saw that the
woman was desperately tearing herself out of her blouse;
she was having trouble with a button; he helped her. As
soon as the button was through the hole, the woman
grabbed him and pulled him on her; she began to fuck vig-
orously and with the power of an animal; his cock got very
hard again, and they both began to breathe in Ah's. He
maintained consciousness long enough to look at the
woman's face; was this the same woman that he had met in
the embassy? The same Miss Smith? The red-neck from
Oklahoma who had only a high-school education; the consul
at the American embassy in Copenhagen? He looked behind
him and saw the white thighs hung over his back; he looked
in his arms and saw rows of sweat, a bead of sweat perched
on a mount of fat; was this the same woman? He jammed his
cock deeper and the woman responded with a scream and
squeezed him so tight he feared that if he kept fucking her
this hard she'd either choke him to death or break some of
his ribs; still, he liked the way her ass picked up strokes
when he jammed her; he remembered that once he was driving his father's new car on a back highway in North Carolina.
He was driving at 100 mph, and he knew that if he went any
faster he might kill himself; still, he jammed his foot to the
floor, and the car shot forward almost uncontrollably, and he
thought he would surely be killed, but as soon as he was past
the possibility of death, and as the car slackened its reckless

speed, the impulse to play with death would hit him again; and each time it did, he played, each time he would jam it; he jammed the woman and was certain this time he was going to come, going to die; and if he did, he would be finished; he would explode with . . . joy; if he came, if he jammed it to the floor, and roared off the highway at 135 mph, if he came, then the numbness in the back of his head would go away. But now the woman was fucking with the steady regularity of a clock; his cock was larger than he ever remembered it being and it fit the woman like she still had her hand tightly around it. He heard some words coming incoherently from the woman, and he listened closely. She was saying that she was old enough to be his mother. And then, as she repeated it, her ass began to pick up speed. He pulled his cock out of her until only just the head was in her; if he had pulled it out any farther, it would have to be put back in; when it was out this far, he slapped it into the woman as hard as he could. She began to gag and sound like she was choking; he thought she was coming, but then she began fucking with the same regularity as before. Then it occurred to him that she was going to come when she was ready. He began to concentrate on the numbness; there was something in it, some message, something written on a piece of paper and placed in a bottle and sent afloat. Just then the woman tightened her legs around his back, and began to release slowly a long melodic line of AAAHHH's; there was that in the melody that spoke of coming. Yes, she was coming; he got ready, he began to harmonize.

"Fuck, you white cracker," he whispered in the woman's ear, and for a moment he felt he had been indiscreet; but then the woman began to come; he felt the numbness loosen up.

"You white cracker, you wanted it, so fuck, fuck." The woman began to cry. He himself was coming; then there was no more come in his scrotum, and then there was, and he was coming again.

Malcolm, Malcolm. You white bitches done killed Malcolm.

He slept in Ruth Smith's arms all afternoon.

twelve

George woke up, and picked up the woman's arm that had been thrown across his face and put it down quietly beside her. Then, it was clear that she was not asleep at all. Her eyes were open, open in a way that led you to believe they had been open a long time and she had been lying there just thinking about something. The room got very dark. Copenhagen was getting old and dark and grim in the dying afternoon outside the window. George put his hand under the cover and touched the woman's thigh. George said it's nice and Ruth Smith turned her head toward him and she looked pretty like a girl, probably not for twenty years had she looked that way. Then he put his hand on her breasts, and she felt like a young girl. He didn't mind it at all that she was around forty. She certainly didn't seem like it. What were you thinking, George said, and Ruth Smith said when; just a minute ago, George said.

Just that I'm getting old, and you're so young and beautiful, she said.

No, that's not true at all, he said.

I'm getting old, you know how old I am, she said.

You were very good. You did it like a young horse. Good fuck, he said.

No, she said vacantly.

You were really nice, he said. He got up on his elbow, and took one of the breasts in hand, and kissed it. He tried to ignore the sag. I think you're really nice, he said, you really like to fuck. There are a lot of people who don't like to fuck, you know. It's hard.

Old age scares me, Ruth Smith said.

Scares me too, George said.

But you're still very young.

Old age and Death scare me, George said.

Death doesn't bother me, it's being discarded by people, especially men. I love you because you are young, Ruth Smith said.

George said that it's when I lie down that I think of death, you know, and that when I'm up walking around it's like I'll never die. Lying down is a kind of symbolic death, and so is fucking, which must be the soul of death, and dreaming.

Ruth Smith said that she would like to meet him every day of her life like this, even if it made him think of death, and then she said this is the stuff of life, and laid her hand on his cock.

Well, George said, I'd like to meet you here.

I'll pay the rent, Ruth Smith said, and you can stay here if you want to.

Beautiful, George said.

Why are you doing this? What are you getting out of it? Ruth Smith said.

George said that she knew as well as he did what he was getting out of it, and Ruth Smith said that she was hoping he was going to say that he liked her or just any little indication of something like that, and then George said that of course he liked her, that he couldn't do it, couldn't even bring himself to see her if he didn't like her goddamnit. He added that Miss Ruth Smith was a boss chick and she said that she suspected that was some kind of slang expression. And he said so what, and that he thought she was a groove and a fine piece of ass. And she laughed, and he had the impression that she finally understood. Miss Ruth Smith said that she had a dinner date with some top American officials and then she got up and started putting on her clothes.

She had on her panties and then the black bra, and then standing up putting on her skirt she looked about thirty-five. Okay she said I'll see you tomorrow afternoon. She took out a roll of bills from her purse and laid it on the table near the door as she stood in the door. She said that that should take care of you. George didn't say anything and watched her go out the door.

He sat on the bed looking at the money on the table. He was nude. Then he got up and went over to the table and picked up the bundle of money and counted it. It was a $50 bill and two twenties. American money. He put it in his wallet, which he had to go over to his pants lying on the floor and get. He got dressed and went out the hotel.

He walked into the Drop Inn and went to the counter and got an Elephant and sat down near the Round Table. Jero and two other brothers were sitting at the Round Table.

"What's happening man," Jero said.

George said there ain't nothin' happening. He poured the beer down the side of the glass. He saw Jero watching him doing it.

"Who's that broad," one of the brothers said.

"Who, you mean Alisa," Jero said. They were talking about the waitress who was new. She had a very fine nose and she looked French, but you couldn't tell if she was white or black. She had a fine dark-olive color of skin all over. She had a pair of fine breasts, fine ass, and fine legs. She was a fine-looking woman.

"That's Bob Jacobs' old lady, or at least used to be. Bitch was rich, man, married to some French cat. Bob took the chick's bread, man. Her old man kicked her out, Bob got her pregnant. Now she just follow the cat around, man. I mean, you know she got this job here so she can keep an eye on him, I guess. Bob's a rough motherfucker."

"Do I know this cat," the brother said.

"He brought them drums over for us, remember," Jero said.

"Oh, yeah . . . I dig the dude."

The other brother who hadn't spoken said that Bob was a tough dude with them Swedish broads and was married to the daughter of some Swedish millionaire.

"Yeah, he's a nice guy," George said finally. He got up from the table and went over to the newspaper rack and got *The New York Times*. He read the editorial, which was about whether or not there was any connection between riots in various cities in America. He got up and went into the men's room and pissed and came back. He saw Bob coming in.

"Hey, Bob," George said.

"Hey, Anthony," Bob said. He came over and sat down. He had a briefcase in his hand. Bob seemed very happy.

"Congratulate me. It's a girl."

"Really, I'll buy you a beer," George said. "You're married to this Swedish girl, right?"

"Big beautiful girl, and I just left there. Just like her mother, beautiful Swedish girl."

The French-looking waitress came over to the table.

"Well, how have you been," Bob said. "Did ya hear the news?"

Alisa spat on him. Bob jumped out of his chair and drew back his hand to hit her, but did not. Bitch, he said, you do some shit like that again and I'll knock the shit outa you.

The manager, wearing a white apron, came over.

"*Ni, ni,*" he said to Bob, with his hand on Bob's shoulder.

Bob sat back down and Alisa went away and didn't come back and George went up to the bar and got the beer and brought it back. He poured the beer down the side of the glass, and then handed it to Bob.

"So what's been happening," Bob said. George wanted to tell him about his own exploits. He wanted to tell Bob about how he was getting money from the consul. He liked Bob a lot. He felt like he was Bob's protégé. But he didn't want to say anything that would lead Bob to think that he thought Bob was simply a gigolo. It was not as simple as that, because he felt that Bob was sensitive and extremely intelligent. He felt that Bob's life as a hairdresser, which was just a front which allowed him to meet rich women, was an admirably chosen profession, provided that one is black, ostracized, doomed, and, of course, if one needs rich women in order to survive. George admired Bob because Bob was a living success in a profession which, excepting that of a jazz musician, which was not very lucrative, was the only profession that attracted him. George admired Bob's profession of lover, because the black lover was a true warrior, a true soldier who is doomed, cursed, to fighting a perpetual battle with an elusive enemy, and with the foreknowledge that he can never be the victor, and fighting every day with this foreknowledge that he can never be the victor makes him victorious every moment of his life. His only security being in knowing that, as a black man, there is no security. Not as long as the world is the way it is. George thought Bob a new kind of poet.

"Ain't nothing happening much," George said. "I got some money from a chick."

"I hope you not thinking of going back to the States?"

"No, man, I'm gonna hang that shit up," George said.

"Good, look at this." Bob held a legal document out in front of him. "Know what that is?" George didn't know what it was.

"That's a deed, jack," Bob said. "Don't many Scands ever get to lay their eyes on one of these. A deed to this house, twenty-four rooms, actually it's a small castle up around Göteborg. My wife and I are going to like it there. Off her rich-ass old man's money. The same money these bastards use to enslave people like me and you with. We gone burn it up until we spend it all up. I'm gonna throw some good parties and invite you up. You say you wanna be a writer, right? I got this friend of mine, a brother, a writer, he's coming. He's got a big yacht. I got one too, or at least will have it by then. But anyway we are going to sail from Göteborg up to Finland. Yes, baby, I'm gonna see how fast I can burn up a million dollars."

"Are you investing?"

"Invest? Shit no, man, when this bitch runs out of millions I'm gonna get me another one. Yessir, get me another one. I invest in myself."

George drank some of his beer.

"You know I just spent five hundred dollars on these clothes."

George looked at the clothes. They looked very fine. Bob was very happy again.

"The way I see it is I don't expect to live much more than fifteen years. I am thirty-five now, and the only thing I care about after my death is my daughter and you know just about how much you can do from the grave, right?

"Man, I think about the time when I was a boy back in Georgia, shit I knew then what was happening. We used to have this saying that the poor get poorer, the rich get richer, and the white get whiter. Man, that's the way this shit is. I hate America, man do I hate that place. I was so glad I left, because I was going to kill some Georgia Cracker, kill some of them white motherfuckers. I saw my old man hang from a tree by the motherfuckers, man. When me and my wife get all the money we got coming to us, I'm going to start a revolutionary movement in America, like in Algiers, you dig. I'm gonna see some crackers go up in pieces. Man, there is nothing I'd rather do in all the world than to machine-gun down some Georgia Crackers. Whew! it'd be some beautiful shit, you know. Man, you know I hate white people with a passion! Now, ain't this some weird shit, because I am married to this white girl and I love her almost as much as I love myself, which is more than most mutherfuckers, because I really love my own ass, you dig."

"Did'ya hear about Malcolm?"

"No, what happened, man?"

"He was killed, by some black cats too."

"No, you mean Malcolm X, man?"

"Yeah."

"Ain't this a bitch. Black cats. Muslim, huh?"

"Yeah, but I bet some white boy's behind it."

"See, I knew he had that shit coming, when he started coming out of that racism bag."

George got up from the table and went and brought back some beer. "Hey, when you gonna have that party in the castle," George said.

"In about two weeks. It's gotta be decorated and everything. I gonna be a motherfucker. I'm inviting all the hangerons here. Every damn body I know, whether I like them or not. Yeah, you gotta meet my wife. She got a beautiful sister, and she'll be there."

Somebody touched George on the shoulder and he turned around.

"Hey, man, remember me," the dude said. He was wearing glasses, big black framed ones, that he jabbed with his index finger.

"Yeah, I forgot your name."

"Bill, man. I couldn't forget yours even if I wanted to," he said, sitting down.

"This is Bob," George said.

"Well, what's been happening," Bill said. "How's the ass?"

"Doing pretty nicely. Hey, what happened with the chick from London?"

"Oh, man, I popped her a couple, and blam, I was in love," Bill said.

"At least for a couple days, huh," George said.

Bob touched George on his shoulder. George looked and saw a very foxy Danish girl sitting down. She had nice breasts and seemed very tall. Bob laughed, and said that he had to go. He got up.

"Look," George said to Bill, "I'm going to take a walk. Be right back."

He and Bob were walking by the Danish girl's table.

"You leaving already," the girl said to Bob.

"Only because you wouldn't come over and join us," Bob said.

"Okay," the girl said, "I'll come over and join you."

The three of them went back to the table. George went and brought back four beers.

"Let me pay for it," Bill said, and gave George five kroner.

The girl said that her name was Ula and then George said his name was Anthony and Bill said his name was Bill and Bob didn't say anything. Ula looked over at Bob and said that she didn't think that he had a name. Bob said that she was right as rain. Bill said that Danish women were very beautiful, and Ula asked him why he said that and he said he was a sociologist from Stanford University and that the attitude of the Danish people toward sex and extramarital relationships and that sort of thing was extremely healthy.

"Just what is their attitude toward sex," Ula said.

"Jesus Christ," said Bob, "are we going to end up by talking about fucking again?"

"You shut up," Ula said. She was very nice. Bob was acting like a teenager.

"Very simple. Sex is no trouble with them, that is, with most Danes, when you compare them with Americans. I understand they don't have any problem about sleeping with someone they just meet and happen to like."

" 'Just happen to like,' hey, wait a minute, that's a lot," Ula said, "and you would know if you were Danish, just how fucked up they are. You know, the women can't remain faithful to any one person. You know, me for example, I have this husband in South Carolina. He's a black man and I love him, but I cannot remain faithful to him, you know. I try as much as I can, you know, it's so terrible. I have nightmares about it, you know. I cry when I see a man I want. I once tried to kill myself because of it. I like men so much, you see. It is a very bad thing, you see. Very bad."

"You sound like a confessing whore," Bob said, smiling.

The girl turned and slapped him across the face.

"You!" she said. Bob put his arms around her and tried to slap her back, but she protected her face with her arms.

Then he held her arms, and then slapped her very hard across the face. It made a loud noise in the room. Everybody turned to look.

"Goddamnit," Bob said, "what's wrong with you mother-fucking woman, huh, slapping me. I come in here like everybody else, I get slapped by every damn chick. I'm tired of this shit. What the fuck you slap me for?"

It looked like the girl was crying, but then she turned and tried to slap Bob again, but he caught her hand. She was a strong girl.

"You shouldn't have slapped her," Bill said.

"She hit me, didn't she?" Bob said.

"Yeh, but you don't have any right slapping a woman."

"The hell I don't, she slapped me," Bob said.

"In the States, you won't pull that shit and you know it," Bill the sociologist said factually.

"Yeah, that's what's wrong with the States now. They let the police and women castrate the men. I treat a woman with equality, man. I don't hit her if she don't hit me. But if she hits me, she's saying that she wants me to hit her back, that's what she's saying in essence, man, that's what she wants and if I don't hit her she's going to go to somebody else, until she finds someone who'd knock the shit outa her."

"No, I don't subscribe to that philosophy," Bill said.

"I don't care what you subscribe to, man. Because this is the way women are!"

"I hate you," the girl said to Bob. "Why don't you leave?"

"Why don't *you* leave," Bob said. "You invited yourself over here."

"Do you wanna let's leave this place," Bill said to the girl. "We can go over to Montmartre and listen to some jazz."

The girl didn't say anything.

"See," said Bob. "She doesn't wanna go with you, man. She wants to be with me, because she knows I'll kill her if she hits me. No, she wants to go with me, but she's fighting her pride right now. Look at her."

The girl looked down at her hands. She was very pretty at that moment.

"Would you rather stay here with him, with somebody who just slapped you in the mouth, or go with someone who'll treat you like you're at least human?" Bill said to the girl.

The girl didn't say anything.

"Well," Bill asked, "which would you rather go with?"

"She wanna stay with me, man, I tell you. And don't you go into that bullshit about masochism. Hell, everybody is a masochist. Some of us are just a little more private."

The girl got up and went over to her table and was putting on her coat. Bill went over to her and she shrugged and went out toward the door. Bill threw up his hands and came back toward the table.

"Come on," Bob said to George. They got up.

"Look, I'll see you," George said to Bill, who had sat down.

Bob and George went out the door. They saw the girl walking down the street.

"Hey, wait," Bob called. The girl turned and started walking toward them. They met her and Bob said they would drive her where she was going and she said *tak* and then George said why don't the three of them go listen to some jazz at Montmartre and Bob said O.K. and they started walking toward Bob's car.

"Wasn't he a horrible person," Ula said. "I can't stand American men like that. They know too much, always explaining and explaining. All those theories about what Danish women are like. God! It must be because he is white. Sociologist! that's what a sociologist is, huh! Explaining, explaining. You don't explain too much . . ."

Then they were inside the car. Ula laid her hands on Bob. "You're a sweet girl, Ula," he said.

thirteen

They went to Montmartre and listened to jazz and drank
and Bob and Ula talked quietly to each other under the
noise of the people talking when the jazz stopped. And then
it was all finished and they were walking out to the car and
the jazz had left a nice aftertaste in George's mind. They got
in the car and drove to the Hilton.

"Hey, youngblood, pretty fancy place you living in. You
must hit something really nice," Bob said, laughing.

"I'll tell you about it sometime," George said, laughing.
He was standing outside the car with his hand on the open
door. He felt very strong.

"O.K., youngblood, you do that. See ya tomorrow, probably. Then I'll be away for about two weeks. Wednesday, two
weeks from today. Around one to four in Drop Inn. Be
there. Bring some friends. And we'll sail from there. O.K.,
youngblood?"

"Good night, Bob, Ula," George said. He closed the door.

"Good night, Anthony," Ula said.

"O.K., good night." George walked over to the hotel. He
liked that crazy ass Ula.

He was going into the lobby when a black girl was coming
out. He looked at her. In a glance he saw she had beautiful
eyes. The Afro hairdo made her eyes look beautiful. Expres-
sive eyes. She had on a very short skirt. Her breasts were
very voluptuous. George thought maybe the girl was selling
pussy. He turned around to look at her. He saw that she had
turned around too.

"Hello," he said.

"I thought you were never going to speak," the girl said. She walked up to him. She had beautifully long fingernails. She had her hands on her hips.

"I don't think I know you."

"Brother, you know you know me. What you trying to pull that shit for way out here in Copenhagen. You know damn well you know me. You may *think* you don't know me, you may not *want* to know me, brother, but you know me. I'm your black-ass sister. You over here hiding in white-ass Copenhagen, think white people don't see your ole ass don't you. But what do you think these people are but honkies? Huh?" The girl had begun to speak loudly and gesture like a madwoman. A few people stopped and looked and then resumed their paths.

"It must have been a *long* damn time since you had a chance to bawl out a black man, sister. But you know, you're still as good as you were back in Mississippi or South Chicago," George said.

"Am I," the girl said. She was smiling.

"Yep, let's have a drink."

"O.K." They went into the hotel and into the barroom. The waitress came and George said he wanted just a shot of bourbon and a glass of water and the girl said she wanted some obscure German apéritif and the waitress said they didn't have that and then the girl said she would have an Elephant beer. Then the waitress went away.

"I was glad you said that about my being as good as I was back in South Chicago although I never been there, but you know if I ever thought I'd have to live in Europe the rest of my life I think I'd commit suicide. Shit, this is a dull town."

"You mean Copenhagen?"

"I don't know, maybe it's the people. Well look, the men

here are fags, as far as I'm concerned. I went out with this guy this evening to the Montmartre jazz club, I think I saw you there too, went out with this cat, tall, huge virile cat, handsome you know the Nordic type, and everything and so I'm really digging this cat and we go out and you know we're having a couple drinks and up comes this other dude, nice-looking chap, and these bastards sat right there making sexual innuendoes right before me. They started speaking Danish, you know, making love in Danish, I could tell what was going on, see. I speak Spanish, German, French, and nigger talk, you dig, but I don't know no Danish, see, and this cat knows this, so he's sitting right there making out with this other fag. So the two of these fags are there talking and I'm getting bored, and this goes on for about two hours. And so I get fed up and decide to call this asshole of mine who calls himself my boyfriend and when I come back these two fags are gone. Now, how about that, *he* leaves *me* for another man! If I ever see that bastard again, I'm gonna kill 'em! Come leaving me some dumb-ass note talking about he's sorry about the evening turning out this way . . ."

"You know you had me thinking for a minute you were a whore."

"What," the girl said, "I am a whore."

"Really?"

"Yeah, I'm the worse kind of whore there are. I'm the kind that *gives* it away. You know, the whore with a heart of gold. That's me, that's Pat, baby. Everybody else all over the world is selling it a hundred dollars an ounce, and I give it away, like a glass of water. You know when you set up a store and you're unfortunate enough to be cursed with a generous heart, you know what happens then . . ."

"You go out of business?"

"Yeh, yeh, that's exactly where I am now. Out of business. Bankrupted."

"So you took to being an actress."

"Goddamn, you're really smart. Now, tell me how did you know?"

"Actually, I just guessed," George said, laughing.

"And so I took to being an actress, a whore, a mother, a streetwalker, a pathological liar, an inveterate hater of America, a waitress . . ."

"You say mother, are you married?"

"Don't bullshit, brother, do I look like I'd be crazy enough to marry some joker—unless of course he had money. No, I wouldn't marry for money! I tried *that* once. You know I ran away from Howard with a history professor. And you know what, we end up in Vienna, where after about six months it turns out he has an immense attraction to little, blond German boys. God, he was so fucked up. Jesus, I hate fags. I hope you're not a fag, or something."

"Really," George said.

"Jesus Christ, is that all you ever say?"

"*Really*," George said.

"Talk about yourself," the girl said. "What do you do?"

"Nothing. Mostly I'm a gigolo."

"Really, I'm impressed," the girl said dryly.

"I write poetry."

"Not so impressed with that. Do you earn more money at being a gigolo than at being a poet?"

"A considerable bit more."

"Which means you're a pretty good poet."

"You think so?"

"I'm a woman of the world, you must remember. And I studied literature in Vienna and at Howard too, you must remember."

"Not so impressed!"

"All right. Where do we go, your place or mine?"

"My place," George said. They went up the elevator and out of it and then into his room.

"It's a nice room," the girl said. She threw off her jacket.

"By the way, in case you're wondering, my name is, uh, Anthony."

"Yeah, I was getting a little worried. Mine's Pat."

George went over and turned on the radio.

"Oh, is that FM? What time is it? We can get some German opera, I think. Let me try. Did'ya know I studied opera for three years in Munich? Nope, you didn't know that."

"Why don't you get a job then?"

"Niggers ain't needed."

"You could try, did you try?"

"I guess I'll get around to it. I first got to hurdle one more obstacle."

"What's that?"

"You'll find out in time." Pat found a station which played classical music, but no opera. The classical music played in the room. It was the second movement of Haydn's Ninety-seventh. Both Pat and George were feeling good.

"I'm gonna order a bottle of wine," George said.

"That's fine," Pat said, "but let's not get too party-ish, okay. You're not planning on screwing little old Pat, are you?"

George laughed, "Of course not."

George ordered the wine on the telephone.

Pat took off her dress and lay on the bed. She had on her black panties and red bra.

"You look very good, very beautiful."

"And black. Black and beautiful," Pat said. They laughed. George went over and put his hand on her thigh, and began caressing her thighs. And Pat said that that was very nice.

George was thinking that she was a very nice person.

"If I had a strong person like you I don't think I'd do some of the things I did," Pat said.

"Do you think I'm strong?"

"There is something about black men that I like. When I was a girl I didn't respect any black man, because my father was an Uncle Tom; actually he wasn't really. It just seemed that way because I didn't understand enough. I mean he owned a drugstore, and was able to send his bright-ass son to Yale and his bright but wayward daughter to Howard, and everybody thought that was hot shit. But it ain't nothing and you know that, and I think that makes you strong. You're coming on so strong now with those eyes of yours that I don't have the strength to tell you what I started to tell you a few minutes ago."

"What was that?"

"I think you'll be disgusted with me."

There was a knock on the door.

"It must be the wine," George said. He went and opened the door. He took the wine from the boy on the tray with glasses and said that he should charge it to the room. George then closed the door.

"Why should I be disgusted with you? I don't really know you," he said. He poured some wine out in a glass and gave it to the girl propped up on one elbow.

George took a drink of the wine.

"Come here," Pat said. He went over to the bed. She took his hand and ran it smoothly up and down her belly.

"Now relax, just relax," she said. "I'm not going to bite you. Now, do you feel that? Feel that lump. Feel it?"

He felt the small lump running smoothly under his fingers as she brought his hand smoothly over her brown hot belly.

"That's a baby," she said.

"Really," he said. He was scared stiff.

"A white baby," she said.

"Really?"

"Does it make you feel a little bit disgusted?"

"Yeah, I think so."

"It sure as hell makes me sick. Now you know why I said white baby even though the father is some German cat, because they are all the same. I don't want no white man's baby in *this* world. Not in this world. I want a black baby by a black man and I want it to look like me and like you with a flat nose, and everything else. You know, I had a dream that I had this baby with a long nose and very white, and in my dream I flattened its nose with my thumb and painted it black. And it looked just like my uncle and I remember being very happy. Weird? It was after I had that dream that I realized who I was, you know. I mean, it took getting pregnant by this weak-ass white man, before I realized that I was black. It must be something in the blood, huh. I mean, I have nightmares about having a white baby. I keep thinking about how white it will be!"

George got the bottle from the table by the door. He poured some of the wine in Pat's glass and some more in his.

"Are you going to get an abortion? Isn't it easy here?"

"It costs about fifteen hundred crowns. I could get that easy, if I could meet a couple of rich American businessmen. Just in three or four nights. But if I go up to one of the sonofabitches he'll say yes, but he'll think he can get it free if he gets me to his place and drunk enough. You could help me. It makes me sick to say that, but I gotta have the money in less than five days, then my safe period is up."

"You don't have any friends to borrow from?"

"All the people I know are in Vienna, and I got enough from them to come here and look for a doctor. The broke sonofabitch that knocked me up is here too."

"We used to use that expression 'knocked up.' Had the connotation of virility, you know. But I can't think of that cat being virile because he is white."

"He's not, that's why I don't want the baby and that's why I call the baby white. Look, come to bed. This wine is making me sleepy."

"You don't have a place to go, or did you come here because you liked me?"

"Brother, I don't have anything. I was just bullying, you know. But now I like you. I want to stay. You're strong."

George took off his clothes and got into bed.

"You got very nervous when I had you feel my stomach," Pat said. She touched his thigh.

"Yeh, once in New York I met this girl, this white girl, and we went to the park and saw *The Winter's Tale*, you know. She was from some mining town in Pennsylvania, a kind of lower-class white chick just up from the sticks I met on the street and took to that play, and I thought she was all right, innocent and all, and then I asked her if she wanted to go to my place and she said of course and we went and she jumped in bed and said she wanted to fuck, took my hand, just like you did, and said feel this, and it was dark so I couldn't see, and then she took my hand and ran it up the side of her belly just over her Venus mount, and said, Feel that, and I felt something like a miniature railroad track, and you know it was stitches, she had this operation, and in my mind I saw this nasty cut, and she said let's fuck, because she didn't care because she couldn't get pregnant, and it struck me as being the nastiest reason possible to fuck. I got turned off. So, when you said feel this, I started feeling sick anyway."

"I've had so many sick experiences with white people. It makes me sick to think about it," Pat said.

George fell silent. He did not want to touch the girl. He was thinking that he liked her very much. He thought that he would help her get the money. He would pimp for her. He would find the fattest, richest American businessman possible. He would bring him to the girl, here to the hotel room, did she have another place?

"Where would you go with a customer? I mean, if I help you get some rich guy for say two hundred, that's not too much, is it?"

"It'll probably have to be all night then. I don't have a place. Maybe his."

"No, I don't like that."

"Why? Look, we can't show emotions in this, because it doesn't involve emotions, see? Extremely business-like okay?"

"White guys too, huh?"

"Shit, Anthony, who else has any money?"

"Did you ever do it before?"

"Don't ask me that question. You beginning to sound like a white boy."

"Oh really."

"Yes, *really*."

"There must be some other way of getting that money."

"You got any friends?"

"Not with money . . . Oh yes, the broad paying for this room has money. I can't get that much from her, not yet."

"Is she white?"

"She is the American consul at the embassy."

"Are you sleeping with her?"

"Sort of . . . I mean, you know . . ."

"Oh, shit, you won't have any problem, blackmail her!"

"Blackmail her? I never thought of that before."

"Just tell her you will. I mean you probably won't have to. But you can. Tell her you need it to pay your rent or something."

"Yeah, I can do that."

"Oh great, Jesus what a relief." Pat threw herself into his arms and then kicked the cover off them both. George drew her tongue into his mouth and felt her wet pussy.

"When was the last time you fucked a black woman," Pat said, breaking away.

"That's a white girl's question."

"No, really. I wanta know. You know why?"

"Why?"

"I just wanta see if it's been as long as it's been since I fucked a black man."

"It ain't been too long," George said.

"It's been a long time here. Too damn long!" She grabbed his cock, and jammed it in her.

"Welcome home, sister," George said, and began to fuck, up on his knees, like a champ. He was thinking, Oh my God, this some good pussy . . . this is the best pussy I ever had.

He lost himself in it. When he came, he went off like cannons, and then his head was just above water, and then it went under. He could have been dead, or asleep or dreaming. When he came to, he said when did you come sister and Pat said brother I don't know I just came and kept coming about four times, four or five times.

Then he was up, searching for cigarettes in her purse, which she assured him were there. Then he had the cigarettes and she was smoking and he had his hands behind his head, like a pillow, on the pillow.

"I know this guy who has a castle, a brother, married to this rich Swedish chick, he's having a party, you wanna come? You gotta come, you'd dig Bob."

"Will it be after the abortion?"

"Yeh, if we can get it this week. If I get the money, how soon can we get it?"

"I got the doctor and everything all arranged," Pat said.

"I hope I can get that money. Oh, I'll get it if I have to kill that bitch."

"Touch me," Pat said, throwing her hot thighs over him. And then they were fucking on into the night.

fourteen

Pat left the room around eleven o'clock, and George lay on the bed. He was thinking that he had told Pat he'd get the money from Miss Ruth Smith when she came in the afternoon, and he was thinking he didn't wanna do it, but that he had to do it, because after all, what the shit did the bitch think she was but a white bitch. He got up off the bed, dressed, held the wine bottle up, measured the corner, and then licked it down. He went down the elevator, and into the dining room, and had a Danish breakfast: bread and butter, milk, and some cheese.

Then he went over to the Drop Inn, thinking that he'd run into Bob and maybe borrow the bread from him and that way wouldn't have to ask that cracker for it. He walked into the Drop Inn over to where Jero was sitting.

"Hey, man, seen Bob around?"

"No, man," Jero said. He was smoking a cigarette and reading *The New York Times*. "He told'ya about that party he giving up in that castle up in Sweden?"

"Yeah, it's gonna be a bitch."

"Cat's gonna have Turkish belly dancers and a whole bunch of other people."

"Yeah, if you see him tell'm I'm looking for him. I might be back around six."

He was going back to the hotel, down the Strøget, when seeing a crowd of tourists surrounding a particular drawing in the street, he inadvertently decided to investigate. Pushing the arms and elbows, he got a glimpse of the artist and the painting. It was a bad imitation of a Chagall, a not-so-bad copy. He saw that the artist was Gloria.

"Hello," he said.

"Hey, wow, Paul. Come over here." He went over and sat down beside her on the sidewalk, while the audience stared, as though watching a scene in a drama.

"How much did'ya make," he said.

"Around fifty crowns," Gloria said. "Jesus, it's nice to see you, I mean, I was just thinking about calling you up."

"You just doing this for fun, huh? I mean, you really couldn't use the money."

"Did you ever street paint before?"

"Naw, I never got around to that."

"Look, let's go over to a newsstand and pick out a post-card of something you would like to paint, and I'll show you how it's done. Okay?"

Cool. Because when you are being friendly with each other, then you'll ask her for the loan. Tell her the complete story. Sure she'll get off 1,500 crowns easily. That way you won't have to go through that old bitch, you won't have to blackmail her, right? Cool.

They went into a bookstore and began flipping through postcards and reprints. Then Gloria discovered something else. She touched George on the elbow. Look at that, she said, and then he looked at it. Damn, he said, where did you get that. Over there, she said, and here are some more. The particular one George was holding depicted three Chinese making love, one male with two females, the whole thing consisting of the most imaginative positions possible. A tongue making love to a nipple here, a red mouth tonguing a cunt there, an isolated arm thrown across the head. Hey, look at this one, Gloria said. A female was fucking a male in the prone position. Jesus, this is exciting, Gloria said, looking quickly at George. George had picked up a book on Greek pornography. He touched Gloria on the arm and drew her attention to a picture of a black Greek god with a dick about four feet long that curled up like a dying banana peel. The next picture showed the same black god fucking a white farmer in the farmer's field. Then it showed the black god fucking the ox. This is the stuff you didn't get in your art-history class, George said. That's good, but this stuff is the best, Gloria said, showing him a pack of pictures depicting young girls licking and sucking each other's pussies. George felt himself getting excited. *Don't get carried way, man, you can't afford this. You better ask her about the money, and stop jiving, jiveass nigger.*

"Gloria, I got something to ask you." George said. They were both squatting down looking at the dirty pictures.

"I got something to ask you too; can I go over and visit you at your place this afternoon," Gloria said.

"No, I don't mean that. Look, there is this friend of mine who's in trouble."

"What friend?"

Briefly, he told her Pat's history.

"Oh, wow, I don't have any money at all. Dad took away my account because I stayed away all night with you, re-member!"

"Now ain't this a bitch, 'cause I was depending on borrow-ing that bread from you. What'll I do?"

"I don't know . . . What about Miss Smith? You are friendly with her, aren't you?"

"What the shit you mean by friendly?"

"You know what I mean, and I don't mean to be smart."

"Oh, fuck that."

"Look, let's go to your place. Jesus, I'm so excited."

"Shit no, you think I'd do anything with you after what you just said?"

"Jesus fucking Christ. I'm sorry I said it, you know what I mean, I didn't mean anything bad about it."

"Oh, fuck that." George put the pictures back and stood up.

"Look, I really like you. If I didn't I wouldn't get excited with you like this. And at least I wouldn't speak so openly about wanting to go to bed with you."

"Don't you understand I'm worried about this friend of mine, can't you try to help me?"

"Okay, what can I do? Rob my old man?"

"You figure it out," George said, walking away from her.

Gloria ran and caught him by his arm. "Listen, Paul, I am very excited. Please, take me to bed. It'll only take a few—oh, go to hell!"

George went back to the hotel, up the elevator, and out of it into his room. On the bed sat Ruth Smith. She had not taken off her clothes.

"Hello," she said.

"Hi." George sat down in the sofa and threw his head into his hands.

"What's wrong?"

"All right, you wanna hear it honestly. I need some money, for something very serious, for a friend of mine, and I don't want to ask you for it because I like you, does that sound so strange, that I like you, well maybe I don't like you, it's just that I don't want to ask you for money."

"The would-be gigolo," Ruth Smith said, grinning.

"Yeah, I guess you could say that. I know you expect me

to ask for money, so I try not to play that role you expect me to play. I want to be free from anybody's role."

"No, it's not that, it's just that you are too weak to be a gigolo. No, you're not like your friend Bob. Bob is steel."

"Bob, how in the hell do you know about Bob?" George said, his mouth open.

"Bob? We're old friends. Ask him, I'm sure he won't deny an old friend. I got him out of trouble once. The Danish government was going to ship him back to the States, and I came to his rescue. I got him the job he has as a hairdresser."

"Really?"

"Yes, he served all my girlfriends. He had a small clientele, but he was well paid," Ruth Smith said, smiling.

"He never told me about that."

"Maybe he doesn't want you to know. On second thought, you'd better not mention that I told you of our acquaintance."

"A very small world, isn't it?"

"For certain people, yes."

"So you don't think I could make it as a gigolo?"

"No, I didn't say that, I just said you weren't the gigolo Bob is, you're too weak, you know, too intelligent, or at least too uncertain of your intelligence. I don't know which."

"But will you lend me the money?"

"You see, there you go with 'lend' me the money. You are only fooling yourself. You're afraid to accept the burden of your role. Are you afraid taking money from rich women is not a *nice* thing to do, do you think it speaks *poorly* of your character? If you do, you are quite stupid, and I really mean it. No, Bob would have said, Give me some motherfucking money, and I would have asked only how much he wanted.

You know, I have about another ten years of fucking, at the most, and that's counting if I can always trap a young buck like you, and I do not intend to waste that time foolishly. If I were twenty or so, giving you money would be out of the question. But, as it is, when we go to bed, who do you think is coming out ahead? Me, of course! Do you think I mind paying for that! Do you think any woman my age would mind paying for it if she could be sure of getting it the way she wants it? No, the only thing that makes me worry is when you leave me, or if you didn't show up. Yes, I was sitting here thinking what if he didn't show up, what if he had gone somewhere strolling with some young girl because he thinks he is in love, or chasing after some girl whose beauty he admires. *That* worries me, and it worries me not because you're not in love with me, and not because I am not as beautiful as your little nymph, it worries me because you won't be here to satisfy me. Now, how much do you want?"

"Uh . . . fifteen hundred crowns."

"I'll leave a check when I go, but I must say that's quite an amount. Mind telling what it's for? An abortion?" Ruth Smith said, unbuttoning her skirt.

"I don't think you're really old," George said, "you think so young."

"See, you're revealing your ignorance of sex and people again; I think precisely like an aging woman. No young woman would have spoken to you the way I did—"

"You mean so frankly, well, I guess not—"

"No, it has nothing to do with being frank, it's just that young women have no need to make the confession I did. Frankness has nothing whatsoever to do with it. Come on, crawl in."

George crawled in, and they fucked like animals, Ruth Smith coming three or four times. Then they were lying together in each other's arms and Ruth Smith said to George that he was beautiful and George said he thought she had a beautiful spirit about things, said he thought she was right about his being a would-be gigolo and Ruth Smith bit his ear. Then she was up dressing and he was just lying on the bed there watching her and thinking about cashing the check and giving the money to Pat and Pat would feel good about him. Ruth Smith took out her checkbook and pen and wrote the check, then tore it away from the rest of the book. The check was waving in her hand above her hat.

"Who's the girl?" she said.

"What girl?"

"Don't be silly. I can recognize a pattern."

"I didn't get her pregnant. I like her, that's all."

"Is she American?"

"Yes, she's a black girl, the only one I've met here so far—"

"And I suppose you're really taken with her?"

"Well, I like her, there's the possibility of a friendship—"

"You'd better come to your senses," Miss Ruth Smith said; then she tore up the check and walked out the door.

George jumped up from the bed and ran to the door and looked out. He saw the woman standing in front of the elevator, and then step into it. He didn't have any clothes on. He went back and started putting his clothes on. The telephone rang. He put down his shoe and picked up the phone.

"Hello, Paul, this is Gloria, I must see you," a girl's voice said. She was crying.

"I can't see you, I gotta go find somebody. Hey, I gotta ask you something about Ruth Smith, the consul, that bitch. I'm gonna kill her—"

"Paul, you're the only person I can talk to now . . . the worst thing that could happen to a person just happened to me, Paul."

"You didn't kill anyone?"

"No . . . nothing like that . . . worse."

"Where are you now?"

"I'm in Cassanova's. How long will you be?"

"Ten minutes."

He hung up and finished dressing and put his hand on the doorknob to open the door and the telephone rang.

He picked it up. "Hello."

"Hi," Pat said. "Did you get it?"

"No, I don't know what happened. She had written it out, and I told her you were black and she tore it up. I'm going over to her house now."

"Oh shit, what'll we do. I made arrangements to see the doctor tomorrow. I saw him today, and he says the danger period will begin in a couple more days."

"God, you don't know how bad I feel about this. Just call me back around eleven, okay?"

"Well . . . okay . . . shit."

He hung up the phone. *Uncle Tommy Gigolo can't even be a good gigolo and help your own women out. What you should do is stomp that white cracker's ass, that's right, jive-ass nigger, get rough. Didn't she tell you she likes it rough, jiveass? What're you gonna do, sissy.*

Then George found himself walking down a dark street. He saw the car pull up, a Rolls-Royce was what it was, he remembered that much clearly. At first he thought it pulled in the alley in order to turn around. Then it pulled up beside him and both back doors opened. The two men took him by both arms, one on each side, and he moved along with them easily. One had a blond beard was another thing he remembered clearly. The pavement was wet from a light shower and the car's lights glittered on the cobblestone. One of the men put him in one side, and the other man went around to the other side. George waited, and then when the man was settling himself in, he let go the blow. At first he thought he had hit the door, but then the man stumbled back, and George scudded right out of the seat over his sprawling body.

"Grab him, don't shoot. Don't shoot. Just follow," someone yelled. *Down the alley. Around the corner. Slow, slow. Still coming. A group of people. Another brother, looks like he's from the States. Hide here. Talk, keep talking. The brother looks down and out.*

"Hello, brother, hey man, I just cop some goods, want something cheap," George says, accosting the bedraggled black man.

"Hey, brother, where you from? The States, man?"

"Yeah," George said. "You like it here, brother? You dig this hole?"

"I don't dig this motherfucker, I don't dig no place where whitey is."

"Hey, brother, I need five kroner, man, to eat. Take this coat, man, for some crowns."

"Five, man?"

"Yeah, five. And if I see you tomorrow I'll buy it back."

"Okay, brother, here."

George gave the brother the coat.

"Thanks, brother, I sho' hope you get back home soon."

George walked down the street and then over to Cassanova. He went over to Gloria sitting in the corner. She grabbed his arm.

"I just almost got kidnapped. What the fuck is going on? Have you seen Bob?"

"Calm down. I don't know who you mean."

"I gotta get the shit out this town. That bitch's playing games with me again."

"You mean Miss Smith?"

"She's crazy, I swear."

"That whole embassy is crazy. I was just almost raped by my own father. That's why I called you. Jesus, I've calmed down now."

"Raped, by your father, Thomas Rowan who studied philosophy at Stanford, who is now in the service of his country and bullshit?"

"The same."

"What the fuck is going on in this fucking place."

"That embassy is filled with sexual perverts, I tell you. I'm just glad he's not like some of the rest of them."

"How?"

"I mean open queers and stuff."

"How'd it happen? I mean, *what* happened?"

"Well . . . I guess I can tell you . . . I'm pretty drunk now."

"What happened?"

"Well, my father is sick, I told him he should see a doctor, but he won't listen. You know, a psychoanalyst. Anyway, I think he is homosexual, at least latent anyway. I know he doesn't sleep with my mother. She *must* have a lover by now, I haven't been able to tell. But she is sick a lot. That's how it started really. I went out this evening right after I left you, and I was in my room and Dad came in and started talking about Mother and how she's always sick and that maybe she would have to go to Switzerland to a sanatorium, and I started crying. I couldn't help it; I started crying and he came over to console me, put his arms around me, and I just had this bathrobe on. I'd forgotten I was naked underneath. And then he started kissing me, and then I was kissing him back, and then I realized I was excited and I just couldn't stop, I—I—couldn't. I always wanted him, and I used to tease him about wanting me, but it was just a joke between the two of us, a private joke. I always had a crush on him, ever since I saw him for the first time when I was thirteen. I lived with my grandmother until then, and when I saw my father I fell in love with him, you know what I mean, not as a father, but as a lover, don't you think that's what happened? . . . He kept kissing me and I thought he would stop, thought he wouldn't go that far, and then he put his hands over my breast . . ."

"You mean he . . . you mean you really . . ."

"Yes, everything, everything," she said, crying.

"You don't have to tell me any more," George said, feeling fear tighten his stomach.

"I must, I must say it all, tell it all, it's the only way I can get it out."

"Well, okay."

"He touched me all over, it was so strange, and then he said he loved me and always wanted me and then he touched me between my legs, and I was thinking I should stop him there. But I knew I wanted it to happen. Do you find that disgusting, do you?"

"No, not really."

"And then he said we could meet like this every evening in the house when Mother would be away. We could live together, he said, because no one would ever suspect us—not Thomas Rowan and his daughter! Oh, God, I don't ever want to see him again. I'm afraid to, I'm afraid, we'll do it again!"

"Maybe you should go away!"

"I was thinking of going to France, to Paris, but he'd follow me there, and it would be even easier for us there, and we would get together again. A big city like Paris would be too tempting."

"You could go in secret? Oh, look, in two weeks my friend Bob is having a party in his castle up in Sweden, you can go up with me for a week or so and get yourself together there. Can you get money?"

"He cut off my bank account for that very reason, thinks I'm gonna run away."

"Shit, steal it."

"I could sell some stock."

"I couldn't get the money for my friend's abortion from Ruth Smith. She doesn't like black women or something weird like that. Could you help me, we have to have it by day after tomorrow."

"I'll see about the stock tomorrow. And, by the way, Ruth Smith is very funny about women."

"What do you mean?"

"She tried to proposition me, I'll tell you about it sometime, but let's get outa this place. I'm thoroughly drunk. Jesus, just think, how many girls do you know that's been balled by their old man recently . . . hold this, Paul, God you're really a friend."

"A sucker, you mean . . ."

George threw the girl's arm across his neck and headed for the door, and then he saw Bob.

"Hey, youngblood," Bob said. He was with a tall and very black man.

fifteen

The very black man had on each of his huge hands three rings of red and blue stones. There were red stones on his cuff-links. He had a big white smile on his face. Ha, ha, his face said at you. He was around seven feet tall.

"Youngblood, this is Warwick, Warwick is a writer, very successful too."

"How do you do," Warwick said politely, extending his huge hand to George.

"How 'ya," George said. "This is Gloria."

"Gloria is some beauty. Where in the States you from, Gloria," Bob said.

"California, San Francisco."

"Well, well, Miss California, how about that!" Bob laughed.

"What's wrong with being from California."

"Well, you know we have our annual Miss America Contest here in the Drop Inn each and every year, and it just happens to be tonight, and I'm playing Bert Parks."

"Ha, ha, ha," Warwick said.

"Bob's just jiving," George said.

"Hey look, Warwick, I know you have to run, so I'll see you up at the dock next Wednesday, okay? I just wanted you and youngblood to meet, since youngblood wants to be a writer and you're already established, thought you two might like to get together; always like to be of help to friends," Bob said.

"What are some of your books, I'll read them in the meanwhile," George said.

"I write under a pseudonym," Warwick said.

"Well, okay," George said. He felt Gloria leaning on his shoulder.

"Well, I have to go, Bob," Warwick said, shaking George's hand.

"Okay, Warwick, see you then on Wednesday," Bob said. They watched Warwick get his coat and walk out the door.

"Come over here to my table."

"No, we gotta get in, Gloria's had it."

"Oh, come on, youngblood, lighten up on Miss Cal."

"I'm all right," Gloria said.

They went over and sat down.

"Here, youngblood, let's drink. What you want, Gloria?"

"Just coffee."

"That's all right," George said, "I'll pay for it." He went over to the bar.

"Yep, man, you gonna fuck right around and let Old Bob pull your bitch," Jero said. He was leaning on the bar with his foot up on the bar rail.

"Aw, man, that ain't my bitch. Ain't none of 'em my bitch unless I got my cock in her honey box, and even then she ain't mine," George said. He felt proud of the way he had expressed himself.

"I know she ain't yours now, 'cause she's Bob's. Look at the dude, man, licking the broad in her ear. Man, you'd be a fool to say that's yo' woman that way that cat's acting, and she letting 'im too!"

"Man, you should know better'n to bring your bitch in here, especially 'round Bob!"

"She's just a slut, that's all," George said. He was shaking and spilled some of the coffee on his hand. Ouch.

"Man, here you go accusing the broad, calling her a slut,

man. She just doing what she wants. Sheet, if you were with her, man, you'd want her to come 'cross, man, what you 'speck?"

George took the coffee and two Elephants on a tray and went over to the table.

"Well why won't you if I asked you to," Bob said.

"Oh, I dunno," Gloria said. George sat down.

"Gloria," he said, "you think we should go home, okay?"

"Youngblood, I'll drive her home. We got something to talk about. She thinks I hate white women, and that's a terrible attitude."

"No, I don't know if you do or not, I was just responding to what you said, which was quite hostile."

"Well, now what did I say, huh," Bob said.

"It wasn't what you said, it's the way you said it," Gloria said. "I mean, you were assuming that I am the average white girl, that I'm just like some stereotype in your head."

"Well, you are, sheet, what makes you think you're so different from Miss Ann in Mississippi lynching niggers?"

"I never lynched anybody."

"That's what *you* think. You're white, aren't you. Your skin is white, right!" Bob took the girl's arm up in his hand. "White skin rapes, baby." He seemed very angry.

Gloria drank some of the coffee.

"But why me? You don't even know me."

"You kept thinking you so different. Hell, what do you mean I don't know you, I know America, don't I? I know what the Miss America Beauty Contest is all about, don't I? I know what my old man hanging from a tree is about because he looked at some ugly-ass white bitch, don't I," Bob said.

"You still don't have any right to yell at me," Gloria said.

"Sheet, you just like all the rest of them bitches. You meet one, you meet all of 'em. I used to think that maybe they ain't all alike, and I kept waiting to meet one that's not just a white woman, but a woman, and jack that was fifteen years ago, and I'm still waiting."

"If you'd stop for a minute and *try* to look beyond stupid stereotypes, maybe you'd see somebody for what they are."

"Lemme tell you something, miss. You know what makes you MISS WHITE AMERICA in bold letters and not just a woman? You know what it is? Huh?"

"What, I really would like to know honestly," Gloria said.

"Okay, I'm gonna be as honest as I can. Let me go back to America and where we both come from, see. We come from different cultures, you say you from San Francisco, right? And I'm from Georgia, now—"

"Hey, Bob, I hate to interrupt, but we gotta get going. I gotta discuss something with Gloria."

"Youngblood don't be so uptight, man. I ain't after your girl, man. Hell, I'm married to a beautiful blond Swedish girl and have a lovely daughter. Miss California is beautiful too, but I'm a married man. I'm not trying to pull your woman, man."

"Well, why are you going through this bullshit for?" George said. "She's obviously being taken in."

"Damn youngblood what's on your mind, man, sex? Is that all you think about, man, and you suppose to be a young intellectual? I mean, you can't talk to a white woman about white America and the shit white women pull over there without trying to make them? I don't believe you think that, man. Look, youngblood, man if you want me to leave I'll go. I gotta get to Göteborg anyway."

"No, sit down, go ahead, talk."

"No, I'm gonna leave."

"Oh shit, Bob, sit down."

"Miss California, if you want me to drop you on my way, come on," Bob said, getting up.

"Yes," Gloria said, "I wanna hear the rest of this. Paul, are you sure you won't mind?"

"No, I don't mind. I'll see you later." Gloria and Bob were going out the door and George looked up from the table a moment and then Bob glanced at him and winked. *Sonofabitch.*

Jero came over to the table and sat down. "Hey, man, don't feel bad. Bob just gonna fuck 'er, that's all."

"Damn man, it's difficult for me to believe she'd do that."

"Aw, man, white ho's are dumb. You dig that shit he was pulling over the bitch? See first of all these white bitches are so uptight about their identity, man, that if you tell the bitch that she's just like every other white bitch that gets niggers hanged, she'll do anything to prove to you that you're wrong. The first thing she'll do is give you some pussy. Man, they'll do anything to prove to you they're not like Miss Ann. And, man, that jiveass Bob is hip to that shit; were you digging the way that cat was baiting the bitch, talking about he been waiting to find a white woman that was just a woman, and that dumb-ass chick eating that shit up, you know she's thinking, 'I'm that white woman who is just a "woman" to this nigger,' haw, ha, ha."

George felt himself laughing. Jero is right, but maybe Gloria was just not accustomed to that line. Poor Gloria.

"And you dig the way he start moving and speaking in slang," Jero said, "making the bitch strain her ears and everything? Man, Bob is a motherfucker, I tell you. He's a cold motherfucker."

"Is it true that his father was hanged for rape or something?"

"It may be true, man, I really don't know, but there are some cats that'll use anything to pull a bitch, I tell'ya."

"You want some more beer, Jero?" George said.

"Yeah man." George went up to the bar and ordered two beers and brought them back to the table.

"Funny thing about all this shit is this: the bitch's probably honestly thinking that Bob is gonna tell her something about herself that she doesn't know; she, you know, probably thinks that he's gonna really tell her how she can prevent herself from being a Miss Ann, you know, she probably thinks he's really gonna be honest and tell her something that you won't tell her, and this makes you an Uncle Tom and Bob a militant. So, when Bob fucks her ass and leaves her there, she's gonna feel empty as hell when she finds out how stupid she is."

"In a way, Bob is telling her that there is no real difference between her and Miss Ann even if she thinks there is one, huh," George said, more to himself.

"Yeh, I mean, you can intellectualize it anyway you wanna, and it comes down to the same thing, a dumb broad is just dumb, white or black. But, man, there are a lot of white chicks who are hip to this shit, and go through with it anyway just to get fucked; so in that case the fool is the brother, you know, because he isn't hip to the fact that this chick is hip to his shit."

"Yeh, but I don't think this chick knew what was happening."

"No, she didn't look too hip," Jero said.

"Hey, man, here comes old Falstaff. What's that cat up to, lately?" George said.

"Pathetic ass motherfucker trying to act like he some stone gigolo, running around with these po' ass peroxide blondes from Brooklyn who lie to him and say they're Danish and got money, and he believes that shit, and these bitches have him thinking he living off them and they be living off him, ha ha."

"Ha, ha, ha," George laughed out loud and bent over laughing.

"No shit, really," George said.

"Yeah, man, that cat think he's some kind of gigolo, old motherfucker, look at 'im about to die of old age, talking all that jiveass shit."

"But I've seen the cat with some boss chicks, though. Some of them pretty nice."

"Those the ones that like their pussies eaten."

George burst out laughing again. "No, man, really?"

"Yeah, man, old Falstaff like them Greeks, man. You know about these Greeks, don't you?"

"No, man, what they do?"

"Man, these motherfuckers have this restaurant, a Greek restaurant and jack if a chick wants a workout, I mean a freakout, that's where they go. These Greeks work in teams, man. They fuck the chick between the toes, in the nose, and shit like that. I heard this little Greek cat talking about how they made this dildo about twenty inches long and put it inside their pants and then go to dances and be dancing with some broad and let the broad lean up against this twenty-inch prick, and man the broad gets curious about how long this Greek's prick is, see? And so, shit she lets him fuck her."

"What's she do when she sees it's a dildo?"

"He never lets her see it, you know, turns the lights out

and everything, and shit she probably couldn't tell how long
it is; and man these Greeks be peeping through the keyhole
and be calling out in Greek to the cat that's fucking her,
'Hey, turn over, do this, do that,' and shit like that. Man,
these freakish-ass Danish chicks go for that Greek action."

"And Falstaff's rivaling the Greeks, huh?"

"Hey, that cat's the next best freak-fuck in town, next to
the Greeks. Man, if a chick can't get the Greeks, she comes
over here and gets Falstaff—that is, if she has blond hair and
green eyes, you know, he don't fuck around nothing but
blondes."

"Man, he's a funny dude."

"Hey, Falstaff. Come here, man," Jero said.

Falstaff came over to the table and sat down.

"Hey, man, what's happening with that blonde last
night?"

"What the fuck you mean," Falstaff said. "We went home
in her Porsche and TCB'ed."

"How was it?" Jero said.

"Oh, beautiful pussy, sweet as honey. I'm still picking
blond hair out of my teeth."

"You bad-ass."

"Shit, you should've seen that bad motorcycle I had the
other night, blonde, green eyes, highly developed, inde-
pendently wealthy, stacked like a sack of flour, long Euro-
pean legs, speaks seven languages, University of Berlin
graduate."

"Oh, man, stop bullshitting. I saw that bitch," Jero said.
"That peroxide blonde from the States, with them green-ass
eyes, and bullshitting about her German grandfather. She
jives your ass about having a lot of money. Look, man, she
showed him a handful of bills and he thought she had bread,

so he took her out and paid for her dinner and shit. That
bitch is on a two-week tour of Europe, man."

"You think I'm lying, huh," Falstaff said. "Here, look at
this. The bitch gave me five hundred crowns just this morning. Here, look."

"No, man," Jero said. "Put your money back in your
pocket. Put your money back, you don't have to prove it. We
believe you. Put it back, you beginning to look pathetic."

"No, no, really, go ahead, look, just look at the money she
gives me, man," Falstaff insisted. "You just jealous; you don't
wanna believe the bitch supports me. Hey, where do you
think I got this jacket I'm wearing, huh? I didn't have it
yesterday. You didn't see me with it yesterday, right? Hey,
Anthony, you see me with this coat yesterday?"

George and Jero were bent with laughter.

"No, I'm serious, Anthony, did you see me with this coat
yesterday? Now, just stop and ask yourself, where did I get
all this money and a new coat, huh?"

"Hell, you probably beat some old lady up and stole her
money," Jero said, laughing. "Maybe you got it sucking
dicks."

"Don't make fun outta me, you can't make fun outta me.
Here comes my woman now."

A beautiful, attractive young girl with blond hair came
over to their table. Falstaff began to button up his jacket.

"Hello," the girl said, with a German accent.

"I want you to meet some friends of mine from the States,
Sigbritt. This is an up-and-coming young writer, Anthony.
And this is Jero who's really from Africa. You heard him
playing drums at the dance at the Student Center."

"Where you from in Africa?"

"Somalia."

"I was there last year."

"Doing what?"

"Just some research for Dad."

"Hey, we gotta be going," Falstaff said.

"Nice meeting you," Sigbritt said.

George and Jero watched them leave.

"That bitch's phony as shit," Jero said.

"You think so," George said. "You know maybe Old Falstaff gives it to her just the way she wants it."

"She must like it freaky," Jero said.

"Hey, will you get me another beer? I wanna make a phone call," George said. He put a five-crown piece on the table. He went over and took up the directory and looked up Thomas Rowan's number. He dialed it and listened to the phone ringing.

"Hello."

"Hello, this is Paul, Gloria?"

"Oh, hi, glad you called. I forgot to tell you that I'll see you tomorrow about that money."

"Can you get it?"

"Yes, I think so, but it won't be until around, say, two; so meet me at the Rådhuspladsen, okay?"

"Okay, lemme ask you, uh, what happened to Bob, he take you home all right?"

"Yeah, why shouldn't he? He just wanted to talk, that's all. You shouldn't get so uptight."

"What'd you do, sneak him up to your room?"

"Why did'ya say that? What'd you think I am, anyway? Jesus Christ, Paul, you're the only friend I have. You know, I told you something I couldn't have told anybody. Now, please don't say things like that."

"Well, look, I'm sorry. Pretend I didn't say it."

"Well, just don't think it."

"Lemme just ask you, is Bob there?"

"*Of course not.*"

"I'm sorry I had to ask that. Good night."

"Good night, Paul, and thanks a lot."

He hung up the phone and went and sat down at the table with Jero and took up the beer and poured it into his glass.

"I don't think Bob made it with that chick," George said.

"You don't think so," Jero said.

"No, I don't," George said.

"Man, don't think she's gonna tell you if she did. She'll lie to you and think she's doing it for your own good, see. She thinks by going to bed with that cat that she's really getting to the source. Whereas to you she doesn't have that to prove, since you're intelligent and went to college and shit like that and already know that every white woman is not a Miss Ann, you know you're a liberal nigger. She'll lie quick to you, man."

"Yeah, but I still don't believe she did. I mean, sometimes you gotta believe people are telling the truth, even though they may not be. I'd just as soon believe she's telling the truth."

"It must be getting pretty late," Jero said.

"Yeah, I'm gonna make another telephone call." George got up and went over to the telephone booth and took out the coaster with the number on the back of it which Mrs. Hamilton gave him and dialed the number. He listened to the phone ringing.

"Hello."

"Mrs. Hamilton? Hi, this is Paul? . . . uh huh, Paul?"

"Oh, Paul, the waiter. God, am I glad you called, I was in bed. Look, can you come over right now?"

"Yes, I think so."

"Okay, here is my address."

George wrote it down, and went out of the booth.

"Hey, Anthony baby, come here!" It was Doc, sitting over at the bar. George went over to the bar.

Doc had on one of his bad hats again, a sailor's cap, white, and made the dude look like he was a stone hustler. He was obviously very wasted.

"I gotta split," he said to Doc.

"Going to take care some more ass, huh?"

"Not really."

"Man, you cats sure take care of a lotta business. Hey, come on and have a drink. Let that bitch wait for it, sheet. Make her really want it when she gets it."

"It ain't no bitch, really, Doc."

"What the hell else is it? I know what's happening; they don't call me Doc for nothing. I know why you're here in Copenhagen, why you, Bob, Jero, that crazy-ass Falstaff, and that pathological liar Bill, all you cats here to get pussy, man. And that's about as far as it goes. And why do you just want pussy? Because it gives pleasure for the moment, and because that's all there is . . . after that there's death, loneliness, obscurity. . . . You're all just like me—except I don't even need women any more."

"Look, Doc, I really gotta split . . . you've had too much to drink, you'd better not drive tonight."

"Oh, man, sheet, sit down." He grabbed George by the shoulder and slammed him onto the bar stool.

He started again, as though talking to himself, "That's

what we all are, we gigolos . . . ha, ha, yeah, gigolos—a
poor man's Don Juan. A black man is a gigolo as a poor
man; if he is successful at it, he becomes a Don Juan. Look
at Bob. He used to chase women for a living, but unfortunately that paid too well, and so he had to make up another
excuse; now, he has finally faced the truth in himself: he
does it because it gives him pleasure like nothing else on this
earth will. Everything else is based on fortune, fickle fortune, and the next world, or a lot of money, which is what is
usually meant by 'other world.' "

"Okay. Another five minutes of your monologue, right?
and I split?"

"Aw, shut up. Don't you ever wonder why you over here
in this place running around like a cock hound?"

"Sure I wonder, but that doesn't change a damn thing,
really."

"Camus was one of the first white men to realize the coming decline of Western man, yet his stuff about the absurd
man is something black people have known for hundreds of
years. Norman Mailer's white Negro is Camus's absurd hero,
and that's what you are, you and the others here. Your ab-
surdity is never more apparent than in your relationship with
women, white women—"

"Why are you telling me all this? Hell, I know all that
stuff. I read Camus too."

"Let me tell you a story about me. I was a brilliant student
at Harvard, got my medical degree with distinction. I used
to walk around Harvard Square, thinking of my purpose for
having pursued my degrees. I became the slave to that purpose . . . Everything was subordinated to it. I had to enslave my individual passions, my feelings, taste . . . to that
purpose, because a 'doctor' doesn't feel this, or that. This

purpose, this label, was an irrevocable thing. Like the color of my skin. Then a curious thing happened one day. I was walking down Tenth Street, when I had a vision as clear as George Fox's, a vision in which I saw myself falling down a stairway and breaking my leg. It was then I realized that if I broke my leg and had to miss my examinations I would have to wait another nine months before taking them again, and thus would not graduate from medical school at age twenty-five, which would spoil my future—my definition of myself. That vision was like suicide. I began at that moment to sweat profusely. I contracted a cold, got an unbelievably high temperature, and ended up in the hospital for a week, flunked my examinations, of course, and in a last-minute frenzy took as my excuse the role of hypochondriac. I eventually escaped to California for the sun, came back reluctantly, finally graduated two years belatedly. I decided, then, that the best thing I could do would be to give up, once and for all, my 'purpose.' I decided that the thing to do was to leave the States, to go to another land and live the life of my passions, make them foremost, and my so-called purpose secondary. I began to learn how in fact meaningless life is, how meaningless are purposes, except when they satisfy the immediate passions. I remember once, we were riding around Harvard Square in a car, arguing the existence of pleasure, when a girl walked past the car with a guy in trail of her. It was apparent that they didn't know each other, and that the guy was trying to pick her up. Everyone became intensely interested to see if he really did. There were a couple girls in the car, and they were equally absorbed. The philosophical conversation and heated arguments were suddenly forgotten. We looked out the window as long as we could, to see if he would walk away with the girl, but then we had to make a turn, and then someone encouraged the driver to circle the block, and we all sat in silence, our faces serious. And why were we so serious? We didn't even know these people. We were interested because it involved us. It was something more definitely human than our philosophical argument, no—"

"Well, what happened? Did he pick her up or not?"

"We never found out. When we came back around they were not there. We never knew for certain whether he picked her up or they separated. It doesn't really matter."

"Hey, lemme ask you something. You going to that party Bob giving up in that castle?"

"Bringing some boss bitches, too. Some Dutch broads. Check me out."

"That's cool, Doc. So I gotta split." He raised to go, but Doc put his hand on his.

"Hey, man, look at old Falstaff, will you, with that blonde. Falstaff is nothing but the living parody of Bob and all the rest of us. He sees her as a goddess, a goddess, can you dig that? That's just what most white women think they are. And we black dudes go around thinking she's some kind of goddess, too—a money queen. I don't want no white bitches' money . . . I don't want them bitches supporting me!"

"But I *need* the money. If I could get some rich bitch to take care of me, I would fuck her whenever she wanted it. I don't wanna work for anybody."

"Nonsense, youngblood! That's just an excuse. The real reason you see yourself as a gigolo is because it gives you a strong sense of your masculinity. Every man wants to be paid for his service. That makes him think he has something special, but black cats, when it comes to white women, dig on nothing else. I mean, it's the *only* way they want to relate to the bitches, and they dig it. Yeah, I don't need the money, as a doctor I make more than most people, but when a white chick gives me money, it gives me a certain sureness about myself."

"About your identity . . ."

"My identity . . . yes, in a way, but more like . . . it establishes for me a clear scene. She is the white bitch and I'm the gigolo. Yeh, it's a good setup that way. You don't have to use love as an excuse."

"White men can't do that."

"No, that's why fucking is so good between a black cat and a white chick. They don't really have to talk about love if they don't want to. They can fuck and still respect each other."

"You don't believe in love, do you, Doc?"

"Shit, I believe in love, but love don't believe in me. I believe in *brief* love, hell, every time you make it with a chick for the first time then you're in love."

"No, that's sexual love. I mean, something bigger than that, something that *includes* that."

"It doesn't exist, youngblood, it don't exist, except in your head."

"Why not, why couldn't it exist between two people?"

"That may be true, but you can never know it, since you can never know if she's faithful to you or not."

"Who cares if she's faithful or not. Can't you still love her?"

"Of course you can. You can love a rock, but if you love people in the way you love rocks, you become a rock. Human love has to be reciprocal, you dig?"

"Look, I gotta go, we can talk about this again sometime, Doc," George said.

"No, wait, come here," Doc said.

George went out the door.

sixteen

And then to the train, the outskirts of town, off down the street and it's late, dark, the air quiet, the houses large, richly guarded with curtains, walls, crickets. It was useless talking to Doc, but Doc had put his finger on a nerve, hadn't he? Yes, but what was that he said: "I don't even need women any more." Now, what did he mean by that? Was he a homosexual, or what? Suddenly George didn't want to think about whether Doc was a homosexual or not, and pushed the whole thing out of his mind; because if Doc was a homosexual, then . . . then . . .

Then the number 230 finely engraved, as a date on some tombstone, the buzzer carefully concealed, rich white Americans! Again, North Carolina with the little black boy pausing before knocking on Mrs. Harris's back door ready to run if she came out (for whatever reason) in her negligee. Then up the yard, long walk, green grass, Denmark, U.S.A., etc.

The door opened and Mrs. Hamilton stood there and then she said that he was late. Seemed pleasant, however. George went into the room. A piano was in the corner near a long wall of windows. Under his feet was a deep-red carpet. Mrs. Hamilton didn't have on any shoes. She had on a full suit, gray. She paused as though she were expecting someone. Come, let's go up to my room, she said. George followed her up some stairs to the second floor and then turned right. The door looked like it was oak, or some heavy material like that. You couldn't break that kind of door down so easily. George felt safe and everything. Yet: he sat down on a long sofa, and didn't notice the woman or the room. He put his head in his hands.

"You know what," he said.

"What?" Mrs. Hamilton said. She had a bottle of something and was pouring it in a glass. It was champagne, or something like it, probably expensive too, he could smell it in the room. She was scratching her back with the other hand, looking momentarily awkward.

"What?" she said. She looked pretty without the makeup, whorish though.

She was a tall woman. A long, crooked nose, and a deep smile engraved in her face, again like an etching on a tombstone. She must have been a woman who had known many men, had ceased long ago being heartbroken, but rather became lean with the need for life. She was not dying—maybe Ruth Smith was dying; Mrs. Hamilton was ripening.

"Beauty," George said. The word just jumped out of his mouth when he opened it. He didn't understand it later on. It, however, occurred to him, after thinking about it off and on for a couple years, that when a word like "beauty" just up and jumps out of your mouth when you are in a situation such as this, it is indicative of some deep-rooted loneliness. He was a very lonely young man in that woman's house. Words just don't jump out of your mouth like that for nothing. It meant he was very lonely, but he couldn't know that then.

"What?"

"What is beauty, Mrs. Hamilton?" George looked around to see who had spoken these words, but there was no one there but the woman and his own body.

The woman turned from the pouring. She looked at him and then gave him the glass and then sat down on the sofa.

She was looking at her glass, and then she got up and pulled the curtains closed.

"I'll show you what beauty is, what life is, what love, and death, and loneliness, and what everything is," she said.

She unbuttoned her suit jacket in front of him. Her breasts fell out, bare, loose, like two basketballs. George threw his head deeper in his hands and cringed. *Oh, shit no, nooo, not this again. No more pussy. Wanna talk to somebody. Can you understand that, talk, communicate. No more pussy.*

"Here," Mrs. Hamilton said, taking his chin and directing a meeting between his mouth and the breast she held in her right hand. She put the nipple in his mouth. Tears on his cheek. He took the nipple in his mouth, between tongue and teeth. His hands flew to the breast, and to the other one, and then down the woman's thighs and under her skirt and everything. George felt his erected cock. The woman grabbed a handful of his woolly hair. Then fell to him on the sofa.

"That's beauty, that's bouuuutttiiiful! Jesus Christ!" George put his hand up her skirt and felt the wet hair, so wet it rolled up under his hand into a nice, gooey ball. Without letting go the breast, George zipped down his pants and took his cock out. He was going toward the woman's pussy with it, when she jumped up, spoiling everything.

"Come on," she beckoned, as she went over to the bed. Pulling up her skirt, she lay on the bed with her ass up.

"Spank me, spank me hard before you fuck me," Mrs. Hamilton said.

He sat on the bed with his cock out and disappointed. He spanked her with his open hand.

"Harder, much harder, harder." He spanked her harder, but she still yelled harder, harder. He whipped the white-alabaster ass before him with his open hand until it turned blood red.

"Harder, harder, kill me," Mrs. Hamilton said. George didn't know what to do, his hand was aching so. Sheet, the hell with this bitch.

"Look in the closet, open the closet, quick," Mrs. Hamilton said, pointing to it. George reached over and picked up one of the whips. He took a short one, a riding whip. There looked to be about twenty there, in the closet, where clothes should have been hanging.

"Beat me, oh God."

He began to whip the lady across her back and ass, and still she was crying, harder, harder. AAAAAAHHHHHHH-HHIIIIIIII, OOOOOOOOOOOHHHHHH, she screamed. Writhing and twisting, she screamed. She must've been coming aplenty.

Then suddenly George felt a piercing sensation himself, and he looked down and saw his prick squirting come like a water hose.

"Goddamnit," he said, almost falling to the floor under the force of the pleasure. The whip faltered in his hand and slipped to the floor. Mrs. Hamilton was sobbing and whimpering.

"Goddamnit, you bitch," George was saying, vacantly, "you motherfucking bitch." He was trembling, he didn't know quite what to say. He crumbled to the floor and cried.

He lay on that woman's floor and curled up like a fetus and cried his ass off. Oh, how pathetic an image, to find one's hero in such a defenseless position!

The first time George ever cried like that, that is to say, *really* cried, was the time, back in Royaltown, North Caro-

lina, when Big Booty kicked his ass. Big Booty was fifteen,
tough, big, and mean. George was only twelve and he knew
Booty was just aching to kick his ass, just absolutely aching
to beat George up in front of the kids and stuff, but George
was always clever enough to avoid it. As it happened, however, George had a bad habit of calling people bad names,
like stupid, dumb bunny, moron, names which he frequently
used to get Big Booty's attention with, but he was careful
never to call Big Booty black. "Black" was a fighting word
for everybody in Royaltown, but with Big Booty it was a
killing word—i.e., if someone called Big Booty black, he'd
"kill 'em," more or less.

As it happened, they were coming along the road after
school, and George was chatting to Booty quite freely about
the possibility of Booty's making George a spit shooter;
George had agreed to pay Booty the sum of ten pennies,
that is to say, a dime, for the weapon, but Booty was insist-
ing quite belligerently on twenty-five cents; George lost his
temper.

"You hear that, you hear him calling me black, calling me
black," Big Booty said, dropping his books and reaching
quite unsuccessfully for George's slick head. "You hear that
slick-head motherfucker." War was on. George, for the life
of him, could not, over ten years later, recall if in fact he
had called Booty black or not. He wanted to stop everything
and explain to Big Booty that he really didn't mean to call
him black, if in fact he had called him that most pejorative
word at all; he wanted to explain that he possessed that most
despicable of habits, the habit of using words *unconsciously;*
he wanted to explain to Big Booty and the others just what
he meant by "unconscious use of words." Further, he wanted
to explain to Big Booty that he didn't want to fight him, not

because he was, in fact, afraid of Big Booty, but rather he didn't want to fight over a misunderstanding; he wanted to explain that he really liked Big Booty, and not because he was afraid that if he didn't like Big Booty that Booty would beat him up (well, he was afraid of that a bit too), but he liked Big Booty because he understood him, understood how he was not so smart as some of the others (to put it quite bluntly, he wasn't as smart as anybody in the school, even the little kids that came in the first grade; that is to say, Big Booty was the dumbest kid in the whole school, in the whole of Royaltown, for that matter, and maybe the whole county, there was really no way of knowing, unless somebody started a contest or something, like the way they found out officially who was the blackest man in town was to have that contest and Mr. Mose Tucker won, like everybody figured he would), he understood how defensive Big Booty must have felt about being fifteen in the third grade, he understood how he must have resented him, resented George because George was the smartest thing in school and everything; speaking of intelligence, George had already come to the conclusion that the relationship between himself and Big Booty was tragic; and he wanted to explain to Big Booty why it was, in fact, tragic, and he was young enough and romantic enough to believe that he could explain it to him; he wanted to explain to Big Booty that it was natural, that is to say, one of the laws of nature, that Big Booty would want to kick little George's ass, this being an explanation that if Big Booty understood maybe the natural order could be reverted and George's ass be spared. What happened, however, is further proof that the laws of nature are immutable, and further, that the relationship between the Georges of this world and the Big Bootys is, unfortunately, inevitably tragic.

Whamm!! Booty's fist crashed into George's chin. Pow! Booty's fist crashed into George's stomach.

"You called me black, nigger," Big Booty was saying as he quite systematically kicked our hero's ass.

George, being beaten as he was, with no physical defenses left to actually speak of, torn like a dirty dishrag, as it were, finding a moment to wipe blood from his right eye, shouted out defiantly, "That's right, you black-ass nigger!"

Heretofore, George felt the audience was on his side, but in this moment of helplessness, when his reason failed him and when he had submitted to the very thing he was being accused of in an effort not so much to vindicate himself as to give himself some moral respite, he lost his partisanship:

"Kick his ass, Booty."

"Think he somethin', calling somebody nigger."

"If you black, he must think he white."

"Stomp 'im."

"Think he so smart."

When Big Booty finally finished with him, leaving him a heap of torn clothes, bleeding skin, and sore bones, George lay quietly looking up at the clear blue sky that hangs over this section of North Carolina in early spring. He looked around, and saw that everybody had left with Big Booty, saw them down the road, dancing in the asphalt mirage, thinking, no doubt, about how George Washington thinks he's white, calling people black niggers, and not knowing about all the explanations he had; how could he ever explain; he never would be able to explain, and so, as tears came rolling down his cheeks, he swallowed, as though he were swallowing his bundle of explanations. And he cried, really cried for the first time.

"I guess you think I'm a pervert," Mrs. Hamilton said, half an hour later, as George lay the wet towel across her back.

"No," said George.

"Well, what in God's name do you think?"

George stood up. He had already zipped his pants up and everything. "Do you really wanna know?"

"Yes, of course."

"I think you're beautiful, I think life is beautiful, and consequently tragic. I like you because you're real, I mean you enjoy your perversions. I have my own perversions, I'm certain of that. I just don't know what they are, that's what youth is about, isn't it? Finding out what your perversions are."

"That's what life's about," Mrs. Hamilton said. She was tracing with her long slender finger some fallen ash from her cigarette. She took up the ash, crumbling it, and managed to get part of it in the ashtray.

"I mean, sex is just part of it," George said.

"Sex is just a crutch."

"No, I don't mean that."

"Oh yes it is."

"Why do you need it then?"

"I'm a cripple, I need help."

"I mean something else. Pleasure takes away the pain of loneliness. The pain of death, of being forgotten. You must know this so well you don't need to think about it."

"I don't need to *think* about anything. I know what I want, what I need," Mrs. Hamilton said dryly.

"It must take a long time to get that way."

"Depends on the person."

"I'd like to be that way before I'm twenty-five."

"You probably will. Why don't you come to bed with me?"

"Will we make love?"

"Of course, if you want to. I certainly want to."

George took off his clothes and got in the bed. "What would your husband do if he found you in bed with me?"

"He's in Germany."

"But what if he wasn't in Germany and just walked in the door right now?"

"He wouldn't dare come in my room like that."

"He wouldn't kill me or anything like that?"

"No, if he did I'd be surprised," Mrs. Hamilton said. "I think I'll call him up." They were lying on the bed on their backs. The calf of her leg crossed his just above the feet.

"Who?"

"Fred. My husband. Surprise him. What time is it?"

"But I thought you said he was in Germany?"

"Yes, he is. Hmmm. It must be four in the morning there. Goddamnit, if he isn't in he's out with some woman. Oh, God, maybe it's the same one, his secretary or somebody right under my nose."

"But . . . you're not jealous of him?"

"Oh, I'm not, huh? Jesus, for the last ten minutes I've been boiling. It happens every time I'm unfaithful to him. I become seized absolutely with unbelievable jealousy, and I know it's unfounded. I mean, I *know* he wouldn't do a thing like that unless . . . unless he knew I was unfaithful and he has no proof." She went on dialing the telephone.

"Maybe he doesn't need proof."

"Oh yes he does. He'd better, the lousy bastard. Hello? Hello?"

George got up and picked up his shirt. The woman waved with her hand, and he put the shirt down on the bed.

"Hello, hello, Fred, is that you? . . . Well, who do you expect it to be . . . How was the meeting? Are you alone? . . . Are you sure? Well, you can tell me the truth . . . You were asleep . . . Alone? Is it a prostitute, or somebody I know? . . . Are you telling me the truth? . . . Sorry to have awakened you then, but I just had to call you. I felt so lonely. I miss you, you know, of course, and I just spent the evening partly reading and thinking about some of our better times . . . What book? Oh, just some—" she read over to the bookcase "—*The Good Earth*. Don't be silly . . . Why do you always insinuate such nonsense when you know I'm not interested in such things. Of course I am alone! Are you alone? . . . That's good."

George picked up his shirt from the bed.

"Well, good night, Fred. I love you." She hung up the phone.

"He could have been lying, of course."

"Yeah, I know but I just had to know, just had to hear him say it. I feel so much better now, you know. When I just make myself believe he is being faithful to me, if I can believe that he still loves me, I can be unfaithful to him."

"But you know that he isn't, right?"

"I don't let myself believe that. That's why I called him up."

"But he was lying!"

"No, he was telling the truth."

"But you just said that—"

She was up like a leopard, her hands up in the air. "My good God, don't you understand anything about life? Just shut up, will ya?" She was screaming. George got his shirt buttoned. He picked up his pants and put them on. Mrs. Hamilton was sitting on the edge of the bed, sobbing. Her hair was in a tangled mess and she was rubbing the palms of her hands into her eyes as if in an effort to screw them out. George put on his shoes. Quite obviously the story the woman had given him that night at the embassy about her husband knowing of her infidelity was true. What she couldn't take was the fact that he didn't care. Jesus, did he know about the whips and all that? How could she think she was being unfaithful to him if she just got someone to beat her? Weird. George was going out the door.

"Wait."

Fuck you.

The next day at the hotel he waited for Gloria. At ten after two he saw Bob coming in the lobby.

"Hey, man, what you doing here?"

"I came to tell you that she can't come."

"Who? Gloria?"

"Yeah."

"So, you were there last night?"

"Damn right I was. You didn't think I was gonna let it go that easy, did you?"

"That bitch," George said, "she lied. I can't believe she lied like that. I just can't believe it."

"White women are dumb. Not just white women. Copenhagen women, just women, man. Hell, we are no different. If you don't wanna hurt somebody's feelings, somebody you like, you have to tell them a lie, sometimes."

"Damn," George said, "I can't believe she lied like that.

You were right there, and she lied like that. I can't believe it, man. That's some terrible shit."

"It's nothing, man, it ain't no big thing, let it go," Bob said.

"I was supposed to get some money from her to help get this sister an abortion. Did she say anything about that?"

"What sister?"

"I met this black chick who's a friend of mine. Got pregnant by some Danish dude!"

"Who's she, what's her name?"

"Pat. You know her?"

"No, I don't know no Pat. Where is she now?"

"We can go over to her place."

"Yeah, I know a doctor who'll do it free," Bob said.

"Really?"

"Come on, let's go."

George rang the doorbell, and a blond-haired guy came to the door.

"Is Pat in," George said.

"Pat!" the guy said over his shoulder.

Pat came out.

"Hi," George said. "Pat this is Bob. We got a present for you."

"God, I hope so," she said. "Come on in. If somebody don't get me something quick, I'm gonna have a baby and that's for sure."

They went, the three of them, into the living room and sat down. The blond-haired guy disappeared. Bob explained about his friend. That's fantastic, Pat said. George didn't say anything but he was thinking that Pat was looking absolutely great; she had on one of those dresses that comes right down over the toes, and she had her hair freshly combed and she was very warm and womanly and somehow the whole room was extremely quiet. No one said too much. Pat was quite lovely, and George was certain that Bob noticed it, although George was presumptuous enough to assume Pat was too refined for Bob to be interested in.

"Okay," Bob said, "I'll go call this guy. He should be able to do it tonight. It's no big thing. And if you want me to, I can come over and get you."

"That'll be beautiful," Pat said.

"Where you from?"

"Harlem," Pat said.

"Okay. When we get this thing finished with, we gonna have a little party to celebrate," Bob said.

"You damn right," Pat said. "It was foolish of me to get in this fix anyway. The whole thing—" and here her gesture indicated she was talking not only of the affair with the guy who got her pregnant but also of interracial sex "—is very freakish, you know."

Bob and George got up and Bob said he'd call in an hour and they left.

Around five, when George had been in his room for only a few minutes, there came a knock at the door. It was Ruth Smith of course, wearing a bold-orange dress.

"I really don't understand you," George said as he took the copy of *Esquire* the woman handed him.

"There's something in there about the embassy I want you to read," Ruth said.

"You know, I don't understand you. Like, who the shit do you think you are. I don't want your money. When I needed it, you wouldn't give it to me. Why did you do that yester-day? Just tell me that. What difference does it make if she's black?"

"Well, it wouldn't make a difference to *you*. You're not a woman and—"

"Well, keep your goddamn money. Okay. Like, it's not needed. And I'm getting tired of this too."

"You mean, it's getting meaningless?"

"That's right."

"Well, that's a shame, it truly is a shame. Because we can't go on seeing each other if it's meaningless. Yes, that's right. I should have known that. What a fool I've been . . . No, not really a fool. I knew. I knew it all along, but I just didn't want to face the truth. But it was good while I used you."

George looked at the woman's face from where he was sitting across from her. It was holding back tears. It made him scared to look at her face, it was so hurt and profound.

George said, "You didn't use me."

"I used you. I knew what you couldn't possibly know. I was under no illusions about what I was doing. I knew you would never love me, and I wanted you to. But I knew you wouldn't. You couldn't, you were too busy covering up your loneliness with sex. And I knew when the sex wore thin, you would come in here and say, It's meaningless. But I'm safe, George Washington, because all I wanted out of it was the sex anyway."

"How did you know my name? You're the only person in Copenhagen who knows my name."

It frightened George and made him shake when the woman called him by his real name. What if others knew his real name too and were just putting him on by pretending otherwise. *Jive him, jiving Jiveass himself.* A pain of cold air skidded across his back as though his clothes had been snatched from his body in zero weather. His right leg started to tremble. How in the hell did this cracker know his name? What else did she know about him? Did she really know about his loneliness, about his neurotic fear of death?

"George Washington," Ruth said. The name from the woman's mouth sliced into his naked chest. He felt like he was nine years old; it seemed years since anyone had called him by that name which lay at the core of his soul.

"George Washington, I know all about you, your fears, your lies. You think your loneliness will go away if you don't think about it. You think it will disappear if you keep moving, moving from one woman to another."

"You don't know anything about me, so cut out that nonsense. I'm not gonna see you again; it's making me sick. I can't even stand this room. And don't try to give me any goddamn money."

"Makes you sick, huh?" Ruth said. She had her head toward the rug. She began to weep.

"I don't understand you. A moment ago you knew everything and you seemed so composed and strong, and the next you're crying. You know I don't love you. Said it yourself. I told you I don't even like doing it any more."

The woman was crying and maybe she didn't even hear him. He listened to the crying and to prevent it from getting him down he went to the door and opened it and was about to leave when she said his name again.

"George Washington."

He turned and saw the woman's red eyes. She was sitting on the bed crying and it made him feel bad and he didn't have time to think about it, there was so much to think about, and so he closed the door and split.

He was down out into the street buying a *New York Times* from a boss-looking Danish chick who had a fine pair of breasts that just wouldn't wait, and then it occurred to him how Ruth Smith knew his real name: the business of his passport came to mind. It gave him great relief that the woman didn't really know shit about him. *She only knew his name!*

seventeen

The day they made the trip up to West Göteborg was really something else; it was one of those unexpected days of weather in Copenhagen that can be attributed to nothing less than grace: the sun was out, visible, could be felt on the arms and face and the legs like naked heat, and the wind was just enough to keep you cool. You could tell it was the kind of weather that would freak out the average astute weatherman because it was so elusive: that is to say, one moment the sun had the rein, and the next moment the wind. Absolutely, nothing less than grace. Some seagulls dipped into the mirror-smooth water as the hull of the yacht knifed through it. The boat was around forty-five feet long and seven to eight feet wide, and was commanded by Bob's friend Warwick, who was wearing white ducks, a white turtle-neck, and a big white smile that was forever going Ha, ha, ha at you no matter how grim *you* looked. They sailed out of the Copenhagen harbor and then out into the open sea and then they couldn't see any land.

Jero came out from downstairs with a bottle of some kind of Portuguese wine. He was drinking from the bottle quite freely.

"Hey Jero, man, pour me some of that wine," Doc said, sprawled on the deck.

"Get a glass," Jero said. He put his hand on the mast to support himself.

"Easy on that," Warwick said.

"You got a glass there," Doc said to one of the girls someone had invited along but no one knew exactly who.

"I'll look," one of the girls—the most attractive one—said.

"Gimme a drink, man," Doc said.

"Wait'll you get a glass."

"You greedy-ass nigger," Doc said.

"Ha, ha, ha," Warwick said from the wheel.

They sailed for another five hours and then they could see land, a small dot, and the weather was still perfect. The breeze was perfect too, and they were making great progress. An hour later, land was on both sides as they sailed into an inlet. George looked at the view, at the fine green land spread smooth like green butter as far as he could see, the water blue against the green land, and then there were the brown specks which he took to be livestock, heard the immense silence, a sort of real primeval silence of the earth when there are no humans around to pollute it. Between the whipping of the wind in the flapping sail and the small sound of water rushing frightenedly from the boat's belly, there was nothing to be heard. No one spoke as they gazed at the view. The green land lay on either side of them like surfacing giant whales.

When George Washington was around ten he had taken another such trip, a dark trip that took him into the belly of hell. It was late in the autumn, and he was standing by the window, looking out at the brown-yellow stalks left in the field after the corn had been snatched from them, when out of the stalks, running like something was after him, came Pete. He came running toward their house, right up on the porch, burst right in the door.

"Oh my lawd," he was wailing.

"My God, what in the world's wrong, boy," George's aunt said, wringing her hands in her apron.

"Annebelle done gone and run off with the guitar man" were his final words before he broke down on the nearest sofa and gave a fantastic cry. The reference to the guitar man was nothing less than a reference to the most nefarious gang of religious crooks that had ever set foot in the nigger section of a Southern hamlet, better known by the local people as The Sweet Serenade Singers. They had been invited to the local A.M.E. Zion church to do their bit, and they got the support of the pastor and the sisters. The colored men in the town didn't really care that much for music, or at least when it was connected with a group of men so obviously handsome and dapper. Maybe it was this non-musical impulse that motivated George's uncle to aid Pete in retrieving his woman from the clutches of the guitar man, and then again maybe it wasn't. Well, whatever the motivation, Uncle Washington said to Pete: Get in the car.

Pete got in the car (a '51 Hudson, of which the town was proud), Uncle Washington got in the car, Aunt Washington got in the car, and then George and his brother Corn were about to get into the car when Aunt Washington turned to George and said, You boys stay here this trip.

George looked over at his uncle and he said, Please let me go just this time. He wanted to go more than anything in the whole world. His uncle saw this, and he said, Get in the car.

When they were off and quite obviously deep into the trip, Pete said I know right where they be going. They were going to Annebelle's grandmother's in Florida. And so they drove for six hours and it got darker, and then finally it was dark. And they kept driving. And then everybody was asleep in the car except Uncle Washington, and of course George. There was only the humming of the Hudson as it shot forward into darkness. George looked at his uncle. He thought his uncle was his spiritual leader and that his uncle was taking him to hell, because it was so dark and everything. He didn't mind, though, because his Uncle Washington was a very nice uncle.

The next thing he remembered about the trip was that he was talking to a little girl. Maybe he went to sleep and dreamed about the little girl, or maybe he really met her at somebody's house at the end of the trip, but whatever the case, there was this little girl and he was talking to her, talking to her about the most unspeakable subject possible—death. The little girl said that death was gonna come and get him and take him into a little hole and hold him down there and not let him out and he be crying for his father and his father won't know where he is and won't be able to get him. And George said that he didn't even have a father, 'cause his father was in jail and he never saw him, and the little girl said that that don't make no difference, even if he had a father he couldn't come get him if death had him, and George said he had an uncle and if death messed with him his uncle would kill death, and the little girl said that nobody in the world could kill death, and George didn't say anything because he suddenly was disgusted with the girl. And then he said, partly out of malice and partly because he didn't know what else to say, that if death came for me I'd run away. And the little girl, who seemed to like nothing more than exasperating little boys like George, said that he couldn't run away from death, because death, like God, is everywhere. If God is everywhere that death is, then God can kill death, George said. Nobody, said the girl, can kill death, but death can kill everybody. George sighed deeply as he thought: I wish I was death. Everybody, said the little girl, has to die. Your mother, your father, your brothers and sisters and the flowers and everything in the world has to die. My uncle don't have to die. Oh yes he do, the little girl said, and then she fell to the ground under the pressure of George's angry blow.

And the next thing he remembered was that he was standing with his uncle over a heater. They were both warming their hands. Over in the corner, or the next room, Pete was negotiating about his wife. George asked his uncle if his uncle had to die and his uncle looked at George and didn't say anything but looked at his calloused hands that sounded like corn shucks when he wrung them and then he said every po' man in this world got to go sooner or later. And George knew it was the truth and it made him sad and angry at the same time. Then he said to his uncle: when you get ready to die would you please tell me, because I want to die before you do, because I don't wanna know that you're dead. No, his uncle said, there will be a time in your life that you'll wanna live, no matter who else is dead. There will come a time when you'll rather see me dead than yourself. When I was a boy I used to think just the way you do. His uncle was now talking to himself, but George was listening carefully, and he was saying to himself, Not me, that won't happen to me.

And then one day the time came: he wanted to live more than anyone else in the world; in his life and the way he lived it he was saying constantly to the world: *I want to live to be the last man on earth*. It was a weird trip. Pete never did get Annebelle back. They none of them ever saw her again. They say she got killed by the guitar man with a razor down in Tarboro County, which was only about twenty-five miles from where she and Pete lived. And they went all the way to Florida for nothing.

The boat pulled up into the inlet and they got into two small boats and Jero and Doc swam ashore, and Bob and Pat and a thin girl with blond hair and some other people were waiting with some horses. The wind was whipping the women's hair and kicking up little whirlwinds further back up the shore.

Warwick was the last to get out of the boat and the thin blonde went out and gave him her hand.

Bob said to George as he walked up that the girl was his wife and George turned and looked at the girl who was giving Warwick her hand. Then George saw Pat and he said how'd it turn out and she laughed. I got it on the house, she said. You mean free? Well, she said, Bob knew this doctor and he did it for nothing, said it was on the government but don't let me catch you back in here with another baby. Wow, George said and they both laughed. And then they all piled into a Volkswagen bus and a Thunderbird and went down the dirt road and onto a paved highway.

The castle was nothing like you see in the picture books, not even from far away. But it was clearly a castle, a small castle owned, no doubt, by some landowner in the thirteenth century to defend himself from his tenants. It was located high up on a mound, and they drove around in circles, climbing the mound. Bob was talking as he drove: This is really a castle and not just something built and fixed up like one. Originally it had only two rooms, huge rooms, a chamber and a hall, but the guy who had it before me rebuilt the interior, put in fifteen rooms, built stables and garages and added a power system; before that, it was unlivable.

They finally pulled up into the narrow road that led to the entrance. Down on both sides you could see the green land serene and beautiful below and on the west the blue sea. "This is unbelievable," some girl said in the back of the car. George looked over at Bob. He knew Bob was proud. He felt very good about the view too. It was a very nice place to be. Up there, higher than your surroundings. Just the clean, clear air. And below, the sea, the blue-green sea upon whose horizon you could see Finland like a small hump in the distance. The quietness.

Bob gave them a tour of the place. Then they sat down to dinner on the wooden benches. There were about twenty-five people, some black, some white. Several pipes of hash and pot were being passed and served along with Danish, Swedish, American, and German dishes of food. Coltrane was wailing on the box.

eighteen

Miss Ruth Smith let her right hand, of its own free will, play along the contour of her ass. She ran her eyes over the volumes of books that draped one complete wall. Shakespeare. Cervantes. Stendhal. What did *they* know about it, anyway? Ah, Stendhal, how stupid to confuse *falling* in love with *being* in love. You don't *fall* in love with Paul Winthrop. You don't *fall* in love with young black men. No woman does. Every woman must want to be fucked by a young black man. And loved. It's already there, Stendhal, you don't fall into it (as you were forever doing). Strange. A white woman meets a black man, and her first thoughts are of sex. They're in bed at the first stolen opportunity. And love? Oh, where is love! Miss Smith went over to the brocaded table and lifted the bottle of Scotch above her glass. The tang of the Scotch gave her nose a twist, and her lips spread too easily. Love? No, you don't fall into it, not if you are white and the man is black. Not if you are old and the man is young. Not if you are rich and the man the butler. Miss Julie and Lady Chatterley were no fools. Did they fall in love? Absurd idea, invented by white men who dreamed of riches and blackness—hence, the rape of Africa? Me, fall in love with that nigger George Washington, what an absurd name! Is that why he prefers Paul Winthrop? Another mask! Jesus, the presumptuous bastard, to think I could not see beyond that. Yes, of course I'm simply a red-neck from Oklahoma who with a few strategic lays got where I am. Not *fall* in love. I was already in love with him, from the moment when I was born and identified myself to the world as white. It was

then that I began to love blackness. And now wrinkles reveal so painfully how much I love youth.

Miss Ruth Smith looked up at the gilded clock overhead.
Four o'clock, where was he anyway? Probably out with that
bunch, Bob and the rest of 'em. One could have, if one so
desired, the whole lot of them, the Drop Inn and all,
shipped back to Harlem, U.S.A.—or wherever they are supposed to be representative of. Could have the king of them
all, Mr. Jones, shipped back to Illinois. But they had been
allowed to stay, and why? As tourist attractions? As good
publicity for the embassy? Nothing like that, since there was
always some ruckus. For none of this were they here. They
remained because they reminded one of home. The Drop
Inn and Cassanova were the closest thing to a ghetto in Copenhagen, and one got private pleasure out of thinking one
was still in one's environment. One's natural habitat, so to
speak. Could have had every last one of them deported, even
Bob Jones. Miss Ruth Smith took her finger, with which she
had been stirring her drink, out of the glass, and placed it on
a bell, conveniently located on the arm of the leather chair,
and pressed it. Brigett appeared. Brigett, said Miss Ruth
Smith, I will not be home to anyone. Fine, said Brigett and
disappeared, as if by command. Miss Ruth Smith rose and
caressed her ass with her palms thoughtfully. She went into
the bedroom and on into the bath. She loosened her skirt
and slipped out of it. Flesh, nothing but excess flesh, growing old. Look at that. How could George or Paul or whatever the devil his real name was not laugh at that. No doubt
he did laugh. To himself. And Bob? The bastards. It was
easy for Miss Smith, at that point, to hate them both very
intensively. Once this womb carried a seed. A seed. A child.
But now there could never be another child, no more possi-

ble child. And she was dying. Dying into sterility. God. God. Oh, God. Blood broke from under Miss Ruth Smith's teeth where they bit into her bottom lip, and rushed maddenedly and frantically down her rising double chin, only to be lost in the fresh spray from the shower. Brigett's body was so young and fertile. Why did she waste it? Why did she waste it on pettiness, waste it on being a servant, a mere servant? Did the wretched girl think immortality lay in one's occupation? Unless it be poet, mother, or . . . God. Oh, God, what it must be like to be a man. To be barren. Or a woman who kills her child in the womb. The same thing. The very same thing. God, oh my Jesus.

Doc let the tip of his finger run along the edge of the oak table. He looked over to where Pat was talking with Bob, and the wrinkles around Doc's mouth gave way to a big wide smile.

"That shit getting to you, huh," Jero said. Doc turned and looked at him. No baby. It wasn't the opium. No. Nothing as simple as that. Wish the hell it was. Doc turned his eyes back on the spectacle of Pat being sweet-talked by Bob. Now, how could anybody help but find this extremely humorous? This fine, beautiful, and voluptuous black woman (who in another reality may be just the opposite) being quite obviously hustled by one of the most shallow men since God knows when. Does she know this? What is she thinking about? Can one believe she is really taken in by Bob? Does she see that George is four times the man that Bob is? No. She cannot see. Her "beauty," "blackness," and the rest of those abstractions, prevented this. You can't see it, while it kills you. Does she know what she's like inside? Does she know that Bob is only interested in what society

tells him he is to be interested in? White Society. Dead Society. Nowhere Society. Society of the Surface. Look at him,
the petty seducer, rubbing her leg with his under the table,
and this he thinks he is doing secretly. Does such a man
ever, in the whole of his life, realize that nothing, absolutely
nothing, is done secretly. Ah, what a clever rule of thumb of
characterization! *The measure of one's character is defined
by the extent to which he thinks his petty acts are secret!*
Does a person like this really think he can hide himself?
What a perfect image: the petty man fingers the flesh *under*
the table! But the tragedy of man is that he can't hide: nowhere to run / nowhere to hide. Yeh, but don't you want
her too? Wouldn't *you* like to have that little piece of hot
pussy too? Yes, if you put it *that* way, I certainly would. I
certainly would like to have a *little piece* of *hot* pussy, if in
fact this is what Pat has under her skimpy skirt. But Jesus
how can you be certain that such interpretations ever jive, at
all, with the reality, with in fact what *really* is under her
skirt? Well, shit you—

"Hey, man, d'ya hear what these mutherfuckers did to
poor Falstaff?" It was George. He straddled the bench with
a glass of something in his hand. Doc became aware of the
music, James Brown's "Cold Sweat," and the sound of the
dancers boogalouing on the floor. George's shirt was wet
with perspiration.

Doc had not the slightest idea what the latest trick played
on Falstaff was.

"Man, them some cruel mutherfuckers. See them dudes,
right over there. Them mutherfuckers cruel, man," George
said. He was nearly rolling on the floor with laughter. Good
God, what was it they had done?

"Man, they had this chick, Ula, meet Falstaff in the Inn,

see. She blonde and shit. So Falstaff takes her out, see. She takes him over to her pad, and starts coming on very strong. Falstaff didn't wanna fuck her, probably couldn't get it up, told her let me eat you instead. Tried to give the chick some money so she won't beg him to fuck her. She took the money and split. Soonest the mutherfucker gets to the Inn, he starts bragging, man, you know that chick I left here with? Somebody said, yeah, did you fuck'er? Did I fuck'er? Did I fuck'er? Oh, man, I broke it off in her. I said, I'm gonna break it off in you, bitch. I fucked her so, man; when I got finished she was laughing and happy as a colt. Man, I damn near *killed* that bitch! So: Jero says, he's dying laughing on the floor, did she give you any bread, man? Yeah, you damn right she did; gave me four hundred crowns, told me to buy something nice. Look, and the dude took out some more money, his own money. Ha, ha, ha. Then, Jero said, man, we know you lying, nigger.

"We had Ula tell us everything that happened. Old Falstaff swore out she was lying. Man, he said, that bitch lying. You wait'll I see that lying cow. Then Ula walked in. Jero said, There she is! Falstaff goes over to Ula, who is laughing her ass off. Bitch, Falstaff says, why you telling them lies, huh? Why you tell them lies? He kept following her around the room, while everybody die laughing. Woman, he kept saying, why you go 'round telling them lies, huh? Why you tell them lies? Ula was laughing so she couldn't even answer."

"Yeah," Doc said, "they sure are cruel."

"Them some cruel mutherfuckers," George said, still laughing.

"Listen," Doc said, "what's this Pat like?"

"Who, Pat?"

"She's the first black woman I've seen in a long time. No, not really. Black woman, like everything else, is nothing more than a concept. And I can see her whenever I want to. But what is this little black-ass thing like?"

"What you mean?"

"I mean, why aren't you sounding on her? It's obvious that you want to, don't you. I mean, isn't the White Girl getting to you yet?"

"Oh man, shit, I'm not into that," George said.

"Man, we're all in it."

"But, you're—"

"Why am I any different? Or any other man? Whatever he may be like. We're in Sweden, remember, not *Africa*. Why do you think we're here, if not—"

"Well, shit, why should I go to Africa, I mean really?"

"I'm not talking about where you should or shouldn't be. But where you *are*. We can't talk about what you gonna be, only about what you *are*."

"I'm nowhere. I'm just floating. Copenhagen is like a cloud, you dig?"

"What's Pat like?"

"Why don't you go over and sound her. She'll dig you, man."

"She *is* nice," said Doc. He reached over and took a drink of the stuff in George's glass. Damn good wine. "Very nice. When you sound on her, what she say?"

"What you mean, what she say. She didn't say nothing. Doc, you ain't scared, are you? I thought you was scared of nothing but death."

"Death, ha, ha," Doc said.

"I know what it's like to be afraid of a woman, man," George said, "I mean, a *white* woman. You remember Emmett Till, the black boy hanged or killed for whistling at a white woman. When I was around fifteen, down South, I was walking the street whistling. You know, just whistling. I forget what I was whistling. But anyway this white woman jumped up and walked across the street right in front of me. And this was a white town, man, let me hurry up and tell you. It was called Whiteville. No lie. If you don't believe it, look on the map. Whiteville. So, it looked like I was whistling at the white woman. I mean, it *could* look that way, if you *wanted* it to. I knew how them crackers' minds work, see. So I got very scared in a very short period of time. I mean, *suddenly* I was scared stiff. I mean, I was kind of neurotic anyway. I didn't know what to do. I started to run, but then I caught myself and started whistling 'God Bless America' as loud as I could. Boy, I was a scared mother."

"That really happened, huh?" Doc said.

"Just as sho' as you sitting there, looking like an intellectual monkey," George said.

"It's just that I've never really known any black women."

"Hell, they're all the same. I mean, basically it's all cut the same way. Ain't none of it cut horizontally. 'Cept maybe Chinese."

"I know black is only a label, only an abstraction—"

George laid his hand on Doc's shoulder.

"Sound on her, Doc. Sound."

"What she find in Bob?"

"Damn if I know. What does that beautiful wife of his find in him? And she's *rich*. You know, Bob is cold-blooded with women and yet he seems to end up with the finest ones. I can't understand it."

Mischa, the young mother, was wearing a long green gown which she had brought back from her spring vacation in Paris. It was velvet, a soft green velvet, and she had fixed her golden hair up in a sweep. She came on like nothing so much as the princess of the palace. She was nearly stoned on the weed, and was now making her way over to where George and Doc were sitting. As she made her way through the couples dancing on the floor—Oh, she must ask Anthony if he would teach her to boogalou—she caught a glimpse of Bob's hand on Pat's thigh. She smiled. Bob's behavior was so predictable that it gave her great freedom, made her seem severed from him. He was gross, to be sure, but she liked the effect her father's money had on his grossness; she liked his gaudy taste, his zapata mustache, his mink cape, and wing-tips. It made him seem extremely boyish, darling—American. She liked these American men. They took themselves so serious at the wrong times. The one called Doc wore a sailor's cap, and yet one could not imagine his ever going near water. If he did, he would surely drown; he just didn't seem like the type who would bother to swim. He liked Anthony very much. One could tell that by the tender way he looked at Anthony. And how did Anthony take that? Anthony loves everybody but himself. Yes, he would love a woman, would probably recognize love in a woman very easy. Would he know that she didn't love Bob? Would he know she could love him? Would he see the terrible gap between Bob's world and hers, and condemn her for being careless? Yes, he would know this, but not now. And when he did, would he ever leave her alone? He was so young, they were the same age: would he ever forgive her? She went over to the table and sat down by Anthony.

"I keep forgetting—" George looked over at her.

"Mischa," she said.

"How long you been out here," Doc said absently.

"Oh, a month. We go and come back, you know," she said.

"I love it out here," George said.

The woman was obviously not more than twenty-one years old, but her beauty—the green flashing eyes, the hungry chin lines, the pale yellow hair, the hanging mouth—seemed precarious because as you looked at her face you could see behind the haughty beauty a horrifying skeleton. George trembled. His mind tightened up. He felt obligated to be as sharp as possible. You could never tell which way she was coming from. What did she want from him anyway? Did she know he was humbled by her beauty? That he had completely lost his confidence? Did she know he envied Bob? What kind of woman was this? Careful!

"I don't mind it, but I miss Stockholm. Copenhagen, too. I think I like jazz too much for the country," Mischa said. She looked deeply at George.

"Jazz?" George said.

"That's the only difference between the city and the country," Mischa said. "Isn't that right?" She was smiling beautifully. She could have been Eve seducing the serpent.

George looked at the woman's beautiful mouth smiling half-concealed behind her long slender fingers. He heard her laugh deep down in her throat. Why was she so interested in ridiculing *him?* George reached over and took a cigarette out of the pack on the table. He saw the woman watching his fingers doing it.

"American men are very intelligent," Mischa said.

"You flatter us unduly," Doc said.

"No," Mischa said. She had not stopped watching George preparing the cigarette.

"What kind of jazz you like? Who you heard you like?" George said. The cigarette had a funny taste to it. Something was wrong with it.

"Ayler. Archie Shepp. Coltrane. I like Ayler and Coltrane a lot. You know what's wrong with your cigarette," Mischa said.

George took the cigarette out of his mouth.

"It's broken. Here, try one of mine," Mischa said.

George looked at the cigarette. It was busted in the side. It looked terrible. Mischa handed him one of her own. He put the cigarette in his mouth. Mischa took out a silver lighter from the side of her velvet gown and lit the cigarette for him.

"Ayler is a destroyer pretty much like the Trane," Doc said.

George took a drag off the cigarette. Why was she staring at his mouth sucking on the cigarette so? She made it difficult for him even to look at her. He wanted badly to look at her, wanted her to look away so he could look at her. Why didn't she look away? Doc was not with them any more; he was not thinking about them at all; they were perfectly alone. Doc's mind was off again, off somewhere like an airplane soaring over some virgin land of thought. Did she know Doc was not with them any more?

"Understand this," George said, "I am a poet, and as such I am aware of everything, every possible interpretation you might derive from my existence. I am aware of all that you may be thinking. Assume that." He sucked from the cigarette. How could she possibly know about the jiveass nigger?

(Unless maybe she got it from Bob?) Could she ever know he was winging it?

"Are you aware of the fact that I'm aching to go to bed with you," Mischa said. No, he was not aware of that. But she'll never *know* it.

"But you're right," she said, "about being a poet. You *are* a poet, but not for the reason you think. Just the opposite."

"How can you know all this?"

"How can I know all this?" She then looked at him long and steadily. What was she doing, pulling one of those American college-girl psyche-games?

"I know this because I suffered, I suffer now."

"*You* suffer; you're rich, shit."

"Before my father started this business of businesses he was a professor of philosophy at the University of Stockholm, he spoke eight languages, had a castle in Strömsberg, and a title. He was the nobility. He was the *old* nobility, which meant he thought the problems of world affairs were his. He did not think the problems of the world should be handled by the bourgeoisie, as in Europe and America. When Eisenhower became President of the United States, he cried. He was weak and maudlin, it is true. He would write letters to Bertrand Russell, his only friend for many years, and Lord Russell would write very sober letters back, but it was not enough. My father hated the bourgeoisie so much that the only thing that could save him was that he become it, that he become the thing he detested. The one thing he hated about the bourgeoisie was their inability to believe in an authority above them. The bourgeoisie did not believe in the nobility, which was powerless as a consequence."

"Where is he now?"

"In Florida, I believe."

"Is he happy?"

"He is happy as long as he can forget who he was, or who he could have been. If he can forget that, he can believe he has always been a stupid bourgeois moneymaking, self-righteous, presumptuous animal, then he will be happy. I do think he can manage that. He is an extremely intelligent man."

"And you say you suffered?"

"Yes, yes, I suffered. I suffered all *that*, didn't I. I stood there over the years watching this slow process of death decompose my father, and then watched it leap at my own throat. I'm still suffering. Can't you see that?"

"Yes, I can see that," George said. What was she suffering from? Why had she married Bob? Did she love him? How did George fit in?

"I told you I'm tainted by my father's (and probably my father's father's father's) illness. This is true. I detest men who are superior to me in intelligence. I despise them to the point of wanting to destroy them. When I met Bob I knew I had come in contact with a man superior to any I had known. But I mistook his cruelty for intuitive intelligence. Of course it was a fatal mistake, and I had plenty of time to recover from it. But I was at the time of this discovery so angry with myself and hating him so much that I decided to marry him. My solution to cancer of the body is to become the cancer yourself. Am I happy with him? Yes, I'm quite happy. My revenge on myself and Bob is this: *he* thinks I stay with him because I love him, because I believe in his intuitive intelligence, his *applied* intelligence; no, I stay with him because I hate him, because he is forever duped by his own stupidity. Our relationship exists precisely because he can never find me out. If I told him I hated him, he would have found me out. And this is why I have been faithful to him, because if I were ever *un*faithful to him, this would reveal my true feelings, my true self. I am kind to him; I have given him a child, I have given him wealth, I make his friends envious of him, I wait on him hand and foot. And all this because I do not need him."

"Because you do not need him," George said.

"Yes, because I do not need him."

"Then why?"

"*Precisely* because I do not need to. I could leave him tonight, could run away to any part of the world with you. You're his better. I could leave him, and he knows this, in his cruelty he knows this. He is beneath me, and he knows this. There is no reason in the world that I should not; in fact, there is every reason to leave him; and so I stay against all reason. And why? For this reason: I will to. The quintessence of will! And it is this power of the will that makes my life a happy one."

"You're a masochist, baby!"

"Don't be stupid. It is the weak will that follows every single quirk of reason. If you follow reason, what use is your will to you? Rationality is not only boring, it's impractical for superior intelligence. It dulls the edge of mysticism."

"Why are you telling me this? What would happen to your mystic will if you couldn't talk to me or somebody like this? You'd go to a psychiatrist."

"I would talk to God, who understands this. I talk to you because you're closer to God than Bob. I could never talk to Bob this way. Bob is closer to Satan. I could talk to your friend Doc, but he is off on his own mystic trip."

"You say Bob is closer to Satan, huh?" George said.

"Bob *is* Satan."

"I don't understand that. What has he ever really done to deserve that?"

"I'll give you one example: Miss Ruth Smith—"

"How'd you know her—"

"We're old friends. That's how I first got involved with Bob. Through her. Anyway, she wanted a child. Bob got her pregnant. She was happy, probably for the first time in her life. Bob decided he wanted to kill the child. Because she wouldn't give him some money. He beat her, she had a miscarriage. That's how evil he is."

"Damn," George said. His insides began to tremble. He felt himself shudder.

"You find that hard to believe, I know," Mischa said.

"Damn," George said. His head felt drunk. "I find this whole place, all you people hard to believe! Where in the hell am I? Am I in this world?"

"And that is your tragedy, that you are in this world."

"Damn," George said.

"You know why I'm attracted to you?" Mischa said. "I'm attracted to you because you're not afraid of me."

"What," George said. "Not afraid of you? How do you know that? Bob's not afraid of you, is he?"

"Bob doesn't even know me. You do."

"You think I understand you, huh."

"You understand me quite well," Mischa said.

"I understand you are quite a bitch," George said. It took a lot to say it. But it made him feel good. He had to hold his jaws tightly to do it. But it was good when it finally came.

Mischa did not say anything. She was turning something over and over in her hands. She was looking at her hands with vacant eyes.

"Yes, of course," Mischa said. "In the same way that Katherine is a bitch in *Jules and Jim,* in the same way as Madame Bovary is a bitch."

"Yes, in almost precisely the same way."

"I'm afraid," Mischa announced, "that you understand nothing about women."

"You mean Flaubert didn't."

"If you wish, yes." Then she didn't say anything.

Then Mischa said, "D. H. Lawrence did, however."

"That's because he was a woman," George said.

Mischa did not say anything. She took out a cigarette. George picked up the matchbox from the table and lit her cigarette.

"Do not be weak with me," Mischa said. "I need your kind of strength."

"Now, ain't this strange," George said. He was smiling. "If I didn't know any better I'd think you were playing one of those games you put on Bob."

"I don't need to pretend with you. We're equals."

"Then I'll see you again?"

"In Copenhagen. Next Monday. I will give you the address to my apartment."

"Please. You don't intend to sneak on Bob," George said.

"Do not be this way, Anthony. Do not be this way, so weak."

nineteen

The party broke up two days later, and George, Doc, Jero, and company split for Copenhagen. Pat stayed up at the castle with Bob and Mischa, along with some other anonymous guest. It was a Sunday evening, and George was up on a bench in the Rådhuspladsen, looking up at the stars over Copenhagen and thinking about the strange girl-woman Mischa and the fact that she was coming to Copenhagen and that he didn't know about her, she seemed so strange and all but she was certainly interesting and was extremely beautiful and if he ever fell in love with her what a wild thing it would be, but he'd have to tame her a bit, a thing even Bob had not managed to do, had not managed to do because what was required was intelligence rather than brute cruelty —he was thinking thusly, when his mind began vacantly to read the news being printed by the neon lights over on a tall building: CONSUL KILLS SELF. George got up from the bench and went and bought a Danish newspaper and read in the headlines about how the consul at the U. S. Embassy had cut herself to death in the shower. He folded the newspaper up into a very tight roll and put it deep into a trash can that was standing on the corner as he went by. He thought he should go up to the room and get his stuff, but then he changed his mind. He walked down the street to the Drop Inn. He went to the bar and got a beer and sat down at the table with Jero and two other blacks he didn't know.

"Hey, man, where's that fag-ass friend of yours?" Jero said.

"You talking to me," George said. George didn't feel up to

bullshitting with Jero. He wished he had not even come over to the table.

"Where's Doc, man," Jero said. The other blacks must have been African cronies of Jero's because Jero was trying, it seemed, to impress them with his familiarity with American Negro accents, and with his acquaintance with American Negroes themselves. But there is a limit to which one can carry this, and after that point it's all flames.

"Were you implying Doc's a homosexual, or are you just trying to be hip by calling him a fag?"

"Shit, man. Don't you know that Doc cat's a fag? Did you know he *paid* Bob to fuck him in the ass?"

"Look, man, you mean—"

"I mean, he fucks cats like you in the ass," Jero said.

Hot flames leaped up into George's throat, and cooked his face. He jumped up from the table and just at that time Jero leaped up too. They were standing face to face. George watched the black face with grinning gapped teeth only a second, and then leaned into it with all the force he could get into his thrust. Kick his motherfucker's ass, he heard somebody say, and he thought it was somebody rooting for Booty but then discovered that it was he himself rooting for himself, kick his motherfucking ass, filthy bastard talking about something he doesn't know about. Kick his—and blood gushed out of his mouth where Jero had kicked him, and the thought came to him: he knows karate! George staggered away from Jero, who was cocked into his Japanese-karate pose like some Eastern dancer with ten arms. George fell back, and his groping hand latched onto a glass sugar shaker. The black bastard knows karate was what was playing through his mind; ain't that a bitch, the bastard knows karate and he knows I know and wants me to walk into it and get killed. Yes, the bastard certainly had the upper hand, just like Booty who was bigger and older and knew he had the upper hand, had it and wanted him to walk right into it and get killed, and there was the smile on Jero's face the smile on Booty's face and damn if I'm gonna be a fool twice, why in the motherloving world did it have to happen every time it happened. Them to have the upper hand. The motherhumpers who were wrong, stupid, vulgar, shallow, wrong, wrong, wrong, mothersucking bastards always had it. Have it, and waiting for you to step into it like a dumb animal, step into it and get killed. Let this sugar shaker step into it and get killed. The sugar shaker came to Jero as a surprise. It was on his nose before he knew it. He didn't even see it coming, it came like a flash of lightning, too soon for him to even realize that it was a sugar shaker and that it had been thrown by that asshole George Washington. It was too late to fight it. It just crashed on his nose, busting it wide open and sending a thick spray all over the side of his face. Now how was one to suspect that a weak-ass like Washington could be so stupid. Dumb motherfuckering fag. It was quite a surprise, really. Because Jero was expecting to destroy the light-ass mother with a couple chops of the invincible K, and here was this nigger throwing glass. Right up your ass was the battle cry, and just like cats in regular combat, who would throw a hand grenade into a foxhole and then wait for the explosion and then leap in with a knife to finish the job, was the way George went on Jero after that sugar shaker exploded in his face. Like a soldier. Like something deep inside of him coming out to defend something. To defend Doc, to defend himself, to defend their love. He certainly loved Doc if he loved anybody, but can you ever explain that to some stupid-ass like Jero. On his ass like white

on rice, for days. Dumb-ass African ain't use to nothin', no
deep love. And so he was going to beat this African's ass,
beat the shit out of him because he was tired of all this filth,
of the filth seeping through the cracks of the sewer. He was
trying to keep Jero down. And he was doing it. He had him
down and was beating him in his bloody face, but then the
next second he was up on his feet looking the mothersucking
nigger in the face, and (BAM) Jero's karate began to pay
high interest. How in the shit did he let Jero get up. How
was it possi— and then his lights went out. He saw the light
in his head go out very slowly, fading into darkness. It was
very clear to him that Jero was kicking his ass like ninety-
nine going south. It was very clear. And then nothing was
clear any more.

twenty

When he opened his eyes again he saw the clean, well-lighted walls of a room, which was clearly a room in a hospital.

"Look like you were in a dog fight, and everybody had a dog but you," someone said. George looked over and saw it was Doc. He couldn't keep from smiling.

"Yeh," George said, and he was going to ask how badly had Jero come out or something to that effect when he realized that his mouth ached too terribly.

"Doctor Jerrell please," a polite voice said over the loudspeaker. Doc went over to the phone on the wall and spoke into the phone and then came back.

"Tell me, man," Doc said. "What y'all fighting about, huh?" George looked up at him. Doc was a beautiful cat, a very even brown complexion, a congenial face one would say, and in his white coat, and the little green pin reading Doctor Jerrell (in Danish), he seemed like a different person from the Doc who sat in the Drop Inn and ruminated on the philosophical problems of our times. He seemed so completely different that George didn't know exactly what to believe.

"I don't really know, man," George said.

"Your mouth ache?"

"Yeah."

"Here, take this."

George put the two pills into his mouth and swallowed some water behind them.

"That'll take the pain away in a few minutes," Doc said.

"I don't know, man, I don't know what me and that cat fought about," George said.

"You really cut up his face badly."

"I did?" There was a surge of pleasure in George at that moment. Why was he so happy about cutting up someone's face? What did it mean? He had tried to cut up Jero's face, a black man just like himself, someone whom he had thought to be his friend. Why was he happy about it? There must be a reason.

"I suppose, Doc, there is a reason, a deep reason," George said. "I don't know. I'm getting sorta fed up with this town, with everything. I mean, I'm beginning to break up inside. Everything seems so, so, shitty. I mean it, shitty. Smelly. My life, it seems so phony. I keep looking for something solid, you know. But everything is shitty beneath. Every chick I meet is sexually perverse or mentally perverse or something. Or, maybe that's not it, maybe it's just they are not beautiful inside. I mean, you believe one thing about someone and then you hear something that completely shatters you. Jesus Christ, what do you do?"

"You don't listen," Doc said. "Van Gogh didn't cut his ear off for nothing."

"But you have to listen. At least I believe that now. Maybe in a year I'll cut my ear off. I mean, I know you don't believe everything you hear, but what in the hell do you do with it? I try to let it come in one ear and out the other, but it doesn't go out so easily. It gets trapped in my system and gets in my blood and makes me do strange things, or at least makes me want to do strange things."

"You're losing your youth," Doc said. "You're just growing up."

"No, it's more than that. It has to be more than that. It's

like I'm growing down. I'm growing down into the world, into the center of the earth, except my head is still above the water, I still have my consciousness, see. Jesus, I want so much to lose my consciousness again. To be able to think without thinking that I am thinking. It frightens me terribly when I realize that I'll never be able to lose myself in myself. It's terrible, isn't it, not to be able to forget yourself the way a tiger can, and still be a self. When I was fighting Jero, I flashed on Bob. I mean, I guess I hate Bob now. Maybe I thought Jero was Bob. He mentioned something about Bob before he started fighting. I think I hate Bob because he is Satan, because he makes me conscious of myself, conscious of my attempts at finding something solid. Everything that I experienced in this city has been tainted by his presence—"

"Everything?" Doc said.

"Everything, and everybody," George said. "Yes, everybody in this town, every black person, seems to be living off someone or something else. Everything but their insides. Black men fancy themselves potent when they can flatter themselves to be gigolos. But for me now it seems that that's only an excuse for not being able to live off their *insides*. What are we doing in this city anyway, living off these white women, these sick white women? You know, you and I used to talk about the absurd man, and we said that the black gigolo was an absurd man, an existential man. I wonder if I really believe that. Because if we are black *and* existential, we're contradictions in essence. Existentialism is a white man's attempt to get at blackness, isn't it. If you're black you don't need to get at anything. You're already there. You can live right out of your insides. That's what I'm gonna try to do. I feel like I have been a puppet, a zombie. Ever since I been in this town. And before that even. I have said things I didn't believe, I've done things I did not understand. And it has made my life seem empty and meaningless—"

"Wait a minute, and let me close this door," Doc said.

He waited until Doc came back and sat down.

"When I came here, when I was washed up on these shores, I tried to fuck everything in this town, right? You know how I feel about that now? I feel like some cosmic Peeping Tom. I thought I was going to get into something. But all I've got into was the dirty lives of white people. It's strange how I didn't think of them as being white people then. I didn't think, except occasionally, in terms of whiteness and blackness, which is a measure of the power of thinking white. Isn't it whiteness that we must fight in our lives?"

"Did you know that Ruth Smith committed suicide?" Doc said.

"Yes, I know that," George said.

"Well, what do you think of it?"

"I don't wanna think about it," George said.

"You were very close to her, weren't you," Doc said.

"She was a white woman, but the part I was close to in her was black. But I consider that part a waste too. The white part outweighed it. I think. No, there is no doubt in my mind that it did."

"Are you sure?"

"I'm only sure of one thing, and that's that a man can get to love anything, even the thing he detests most in the world. A black man can, if he allows himself, love a white woman, and that's the tragedy of life—"

"And the beauty, too, George," Doc said.

"And a man can love a man and not need a woman?"

"Yes."

"No. It is a tragedy if a black man lets himself love something in white women, just as it is if a man lets himself be fucked by another man, and it is not beautiful because it is based on a weak will. Somebody must have a strong enough will to set standards, to set up a guideline, or we won't be able to tell who's black and who's white, or who's man and who's woman."

"What's wrong with that?"

"Because I'm black and a man and that's my identity. If somebody comes up to me and tells me I'm white and a woman—a white woman, then I lose my identity, my existence, my meaning, and my life becomes petty, meaningless, immoral, and useless, I die. And I don't want to die, I want to live."

"And so you're going back to America?"

"As soon as I can get some bread together."

"And what are you going to do there? Start a revolution?"

"I was thinking that I would return to the dirt farm where I came from. And farm; but I know I won't do that. I was thinking that I'd write a novel, a book about the race problem with a dynamite stick concealed inside it. I mean, a *real* stick of dynamite, so that when liberal ass crackers picked up the book, which *Saturday Review* will have dubbed 'a searing blast from the depths . . . slashing . . . dynamite,' well, when that cracker opens up my book it'll go off and take his motherfucking head with it. I won't mind writing a book, but I'd hate to be a black author in America. Before I'd do that, I'd be like that flunky, what's his name, Warwick, and use a pseudonym and let everybody think I was white or something."

"Man, you outa your mind," Doc laughed.

"No, man, I'm serious. I would like to write a serious book, but because I'm black, America wouldn't let me. All the publishers are interested in selling books and if you say something about sex and being a nigger then you got a bestseller. The second book I'd like to write would be a book about seven hundred pages thick, see. And this book would have a regular jacket cover and all, except when you opened it you'd discover that each page, each of the seven hundred pages, was empty, except for this phrase: KISS MY BLACK ASS. On every page you could read in bold print KISS MY BLACK ASS, and at the bottom I'd have a footnote reading: MY BLACK BALLS TOO."

Doc thought all this was funny.

"No, man, I'm serious. And I'd get Marshall McLuhan to write a preface, like having Jean-Paul Sartre writing an introduction to Fanon's *The Wretched of the Earth*. McLuhan's preface would be very short: 'White America: I ask you to kiss this black ass.' Every liberal would go around reading the book and not understand the one single line in it, you know. So I'd be asked to go to universities and the Elks Clubs and ladies' teas to explain it. And I'll tell them the book is autobiographical, and that it reflects a black man's struggle to live in white society."

"I like your first book better, the one with the stick of dynamite in it."

"Yeh, it'll really blow their minds, dumb mothers!"

"So you going back to Charlie country," Doc said.

"It's all Charlie country, I'm just going back to where the territory, the terrain, the battleground is a bit more familiar," George said.

Doc put a hand on George's knee. "If you need to borrow some money, stop by my apartment tonight," Doc said.

George felt the hand slide up his leg. He didn't know quite what to say. He moved his leg.

"Things are very strange," George said, finally. "Sometimes I don't know where I am, I—I—"

"Don't be naïve," Doc said. "Like everything else, naïveté is only a role."

"Some people may need to play it," George said.

"This may be true," Doc said. "Here is my address. As a friend, I would like to do you this favor."

"That's cool," George said, and he got up and went toward the door. He had a large bandage across his head. He felt it as he went out the door. It felt like a rock which was about the size of an egg.

In a few minutes George was walking down a street that was as dark as some alley. He felt dejected, and then he felt beautiful inside. He was going back home! But how in the hell was he going to *get* there!

He met Mischa, as was planned, on a Monday afternoon. It was a strange, starkly strident day, gray in the sky, and desolate on the peopleless streets. They sat in a restaurant, over coffee, staring intermittently at each other and out the window at the hopeless weather.

Mischa said, "Bob has gone off somewhere to the south with Pat." George looked at her. What did *that* mean? They were *both* shallow. They deserve each other, don't they. The thing (beauty?) that frightened him in Mischa did not frighten him any more. He looked closely into the girl's green eyes, allowed his eyes to put her blond hair in another context. Yes, it was true she could be some secretary in Oakland, California. Another stupid *white* woman! Why hadn't the simple fact of her color occurred to him before? Was it that simple? Another bitch ready to prevent a man from living from out of the insides of himself, another harpy eager to inflame the world with chaos! Live out of your own insides, stupid white bitch!

"Bob is a white devil," George said, "and you're as full of as much bullshit as he is."

"Men demand two things in a woman," Mischa said, "that they don't cry, and they don't get angry."

"I'm not trying to get you angry, and you're certainly not the kind to cry."

"Don't flatter yourself by thinking you can get me to be angry."

"I wasn't trying to—Jesus, you're vicious, aren't you. I wouldn't want to get you angry, your kind of angry is nihilistic."

"There. You are soft already; you're no game. You are afraid of me!"

George grabbed her arm. "Let's cut out the bullshit, you stupid white woman!"

"What? Are you crazy?" Mischa said.

"What do you want from me? What can I give you? What can you give me? I need money. Can you give me that?"

"I can give you more than money," Mischa said. "Please let go my arm."

George wouldn't let her arm loose. "In America, you could scream, you know, and the cops would come arunning ready to beat the nigger's head."

"Don't give me that, I wouldn't."

"That's not the point—the point is that you *could*. That option has been provided for you."

"Why," Mischa said, quietly, defeatedly, sulkingly, "did you have to do that, to say all that?"

"Because that's where my mind is," George said, "in America. I'm going home, so I might as well start getting in shape, right?"

"You mean you are leaving for America? Soon?"

"Like as soon as I can get enough money for a ticket."

"How much do you need? Here, take this," Mischa said.

"No, I don't need your money," George said, and got up from the table and left the restaurant without looking back. He walked down the street, and then stopped: Jiveass Nigger, that broad was gonna give you some bread you badly need, and you were foolish enough not to take it. Go back and find that broad, man, and get that bread, 'cause that's the only way you can say you won. The rest is all jive. George turned and rushed back to the restaurant, but Mischa was not there. He went out into the street to look, but she had disappeared. Damn. George went and made a telephone call to the embassy and told the receptionist that he had no money and wanted to get home and the receptionist said that the embassy could only assist in having him shipped back to America, the fare for which he'd have to pay back later. That's cool, George said, that's very, very cool.

epilogue

An Epiphanic Conclusion of Some Important Matters

You think that your acts have been lies because you have been acting like a white hero in some white man's novel. But you need to realize that your creator is not some white man, but a black brother, a nigger, a jiveass very much like yourself. And if you chose to see only blackness, that doesn't mean you're blind; it means only that you are living out of your insides, living out of where you first began.

Ah, even this, in the final analysis, even this is jive. All is jive.

Blackness: keeping on keeping on. Cleanliness. Strong will. True identity. Return to Origin. The smell of the straightening comb. And plaited hair and cotton underwear. Black beauty. A very moving beginning. But you can go farther. You must.

You eavesdrop on yourself, you hear yourself in another room making quiet love to elegant ladies. Some white, some colored, some black, or green, or whatever. You see yourself through a keyhole unbuttoning your pants for some degenerate white lady. You peep from under the table and see yourself talking money to a white publisher. In another room you hear yourself telling a black man that your real name is . . . you see yourself scratch your woolly head trying to remember. Then you remember but it is too late. It was probably lost on him anyway.

Ah, even this, in the final analysis, even this is jive. All is jive.

Circles. Everybody moving in circles. And talking in them too. Circus. Everybody talking in circuses like talking dogs

who have only a few words to say. You wanna be something.
And stop wasting whatever it is that you are wasting. There
comes that time. It is called "The End." You know the Atlan-
tic Ocean is beneath your feet. You know you are going
home. Home. Home. Home? Home! O.K. And you know it
could be your mother's womb (or your father's). But assume
you decide to die. So you present your body as having been
riddled by life. Now watch.

The little old man who looks like a newspaperman is a
newspaperman. He will look at your dead head and say you
were mentally deranged. His twenty-three-year-old niece, a
sociology student at the University of Chicago, will look at
your dying biceps and say something exactingly sociological.
They will interpret your ass nigger. Knowing they will have
it all wrong. And will not believe you when you rise from the
grave on the day of resurrection.

But they need to understand you. Need to. If they fail to
understand how you live they'll "kill" your ass, and call you a
"dead man." Which, incidentally, is the way they classify
everything they "kill."

As sure as you are a jiveass nigger, some well-meaning
intellectuals will be picking through your soul—ha, ha, ha,
what they believe to be your soul—will be picking through
your dirty drawers, and undoubtedly some frail lady will
turn your dead cock over with the tip of her Scripto looking
for "meaning." But they will not find it here, not the same
meaning they find in fine "homes" in the Berkeley hills, Wall
Street, Pepsi-Cola, Perry Como, toilets, Nixon, crew cuts,
and Cadillacs. You will have them understand what you
mean by jive.